THE ANIMALS
v.
SAMUEL WILLIS

Will Lowrey

THE ANIMALS v. SAMUEL WILLIS
Copyright © 2020 by William C. Lowrey

First Edition

Editing by Lana Mowdy
Cover by Youness LH
Formatting by The Book Khaleesi

Published by Lomack Publishing
ISBN: 978-1-7329399-6-7

www.lomackpublishing.com

ALSO BY WILL LOWREY

Chasing the Blue Sky

Where the Irises Bloom

The Tenebrous Mind

Words on a Killing

Odd Robert

Simple Strategies for the Bar Exam

For all those who will never know
the light of a new day.

*"Rather than love, than money, than fame,
give me truth."*

Henry David Thoreau

CHAPTER 1

Perched high above the venerable court-room on claws and hooves, the denizens of Plum Grove bustled with anticipation. Occasionally, tufts of fur and feathers shook loose and wafted lazily from the balcony to the weathered maple floor below as the animals pushed and pressed for seating in the cramped space. All about the courtroom, a palpable buzz lingered in the stale, late-summer air as fowl and mammal alike contended vigorously for the best seat to the day's event.

Seated below, at a bland, rectangular oak table, Millard P. Tibbitts peered down, diligently shuffling papers across the desk with his maize beak. Tibbitts rested comfortably atop a hard wooden chair; another sat lonely and empty beside him. He would work alone today, just as he preferred.

As the most prominent rooster in the tiny town of Plum Grove, Tibbitts was well-known and regarded as something of a maverick. Even before the great emancipation, he could be seen parading through town on his own accord, the lush, amber feathers on his chest puffed regally for all to see. Though formally owned by the ailing widow, Miss Rose Davenport, Tibbitts was long-considered no one's property. Each morning, the old bird would rise in the ramshackle coop on the dilapidated Davenport farm at the edge of town and crow vociferously before beginning his regular saunter through the streets of Plum Grove.

In the years since Miss Davenport's husband fell ill and passed, the small farm had fallen into grave disrepair, the vines weaving serpent-like around the once-stately pillars and the old hexagonal wire fence crumbling and toppling in places. Tibbitts wasted no time taking advantage of the decrepit conditions and, before long, had broached the old fence and made his way into town. At first, the humans chided and jeered at him, sometimes poking at him with great straw brooms to shoo him back from whence he came. The old bird was relentless, though. When pressed too firmly, he would scuttle after the offender, flapping his broad wings powerfully. Eventually, their resolve faltered, and they left the bird to his druthers where he mingled among them, though leery eyes always followed.

A few paces to Tibbitts' right in the courtrroom,

Cyrus Sutton, or "Boots" as he was colloquially known, padded back and forth behind a rectangular table of his own, his white paws treading silently across the hardwood floor. Occasionally, the cat's slate-gray tail swished theatrically, and his deep, flaxen eyes narrowed to slits as he looked out impatiently on the crowd gathering on the ground floor beyond the low wooden railing that separated the well of the courtroom from the gallery.

Just on the other side of the blanched white railing, a throng of humans gathered, their size equaling the bustling masses of animals above in the balcony, but much more subdued. In the rows of hard, wooden benches behind Cyrus' table, every seat was filled — mostly weathered, stone-faced men in dungarees, overalls, and faded plaid shirts. On their laps, straw and felt hats coated with dust from the fields rested, somewhat out of place in the old courtroom.

Across the aisle, behind Tibbitts, the gallery brimmed with black and white Holsteins, resting uncomfortably on their haunches on the edges of the wooden benches. Mixed in with the weighty cows was a small number of other farm animals — a pair of geese, a flock of chickens, a smattering of goats, a pig, some mangy dogs, and an old donkey standing dolefully near the door.

THE ANIMALS v. SAMUEL WILLIS

The courtroom swelled with unmistakable buzz of anticipation, and despite his outwardly cool nature, Cyrus was on edge. Just weeks ago, the animals of the farms had been emancipated. After generations of toiling in the fields at the end of whips, strapped broken-backed to plows, and stowed away in the cold, muddy confines of birthing sheds, a new day had come and the old ways were no longer.

In the few, uneasy days that followed, the farm animals had brought forward the present case —almost as if they had this planned all along — a simple case about a simple man. Yet, today was about so much more.

In the rear of the courtroom, just beside the tall, angular judge's bench that loomed above the courtroom from a small pedestal, a wooden door creaked open. From the shadows beyond the doorway, a leathery black snout poked cautiously into the courtroom, followed by a pair of coal-black eyes set amidst a coat of long, cream colored fur. The massive bailiff dog scanned the room, ensuring the crowd had taken their seats. For a moment, he watched silently, his snout conspicuously poking into the room.

After a few brief seconds, the crowd noticed him, and a deathly hush quickly fell over the room as the last animals pushed into the few open seats behind Tibbitts. When the courtroom was silent, the bailiff dog stepped from the shadows on giant paws and stood like a sentinel before the crowd. To his right, the jury box rose slightly from a small platform, seven straight-backed wooden chairs surrounded by crisp white railing. To the dog's left stood the judge's position, an ornate oak chair resting behind a three-sided bench.

For a few anxious moments, the bailiff dog stood beside the judge's bench until nary a finger or claw moved in the courtroom. Solemnly, he waited until the last feather drifted softly from the balcony above, landing on a sour-faced farmer below. With scantly hidden disdain, the farmer roughly swept his hand over his sleeve and brushed the feather to the floor, his eyes darting upward like daggers at the unseen creatures above.

Finally, the bailiff dog spoke. "All rise!" he bellowed, his deep baritone casting across the small courtroom and resounding off the wooden walls. "The Honorable Rayford Q. Fogel presiding!"

Claws and hooves scratched on the wooden floor as the animals rose, drowning out the squeaking of the farmer's boots. Behind the bailiff dog, the wooden door cracked once more and opened wide. For a brief second, there was complete silence and then the sound of hooves clicking on the hardwood floor in a slow, deliberate cadence.

Out of the murky shadows, The Honorable Rayford Q. Fogel emerged, his wizened, snow-white face appearing through the doorway, a pair of cloudy, onyx eyes set behind a bony white snout. A dark, makeshift robe covered a long coat of wool that shown through in ragged patches of dingy gray. Judge Fogel slowly approached the bench, methodically climbing the three steps. When he reached the chair, he placed his front hooves up first and hopped upward with a vigor that belied his old age. Resting atop the ornate chair, he sat back on his haunches, and then slowly, he lifted his head, surveying the court-room for the first time.

For a long moment, the courtroom was silent as Judge Fogel allowed the last of the creaks to drain from the old bench. Finally, he spoke. "You may be seated," he said, his voice authoritative yet low in a way that demanded careful attention.

In the balcony beyond the white bannisters and in the gallery below, men and animals slowly bent their joints and rested on their haunches or simply perched at the edge of the hard, wooden benches. Behind Cyrus, a faint muttering stirred within the congregation of humans pressed to-gether in anxious anticipation.

At the head of the courtroom, Judge Fogel sat quietly, letting the crowd settle. When the shuffling and scratching of claws on hardwood had passed, the courtroom grew silent save for the quiet mumbling of a pair of dingy farmers seated near the back row. Judge Fogel's coal-black eyes gazed straight ahead, over Cyrus, and into the gallery. With a cold, silent stare, he waited, well-aware that the eyes of the crowd lingered upon him. The muttering continued — a few brusque, oblivious whispers between the two men, heads bowed and unaware of Judge Fogel's attention.

Cyrus darted his eyes upward from the papers on his desk and saw Judge Fogel looking stoically into the crowd. Then he followed the old sheep's eyes into the gallery where the pair of farmers conversed obliviously.

"Gentlemen," spoke Judge Fogel, his tone firm and grave. Hooves squeaked on the hardwood as animals shuffled uncomfortably. The Holsteins turned and looked across the aisle into the other side of the gallery as the two farmers suddenly lifted their heads, slack-jawed, and stared ahead in surprise. One of them, an older man with stringy gray hair like rotten, rain-soaked straw, scanned the courtroom, unable to mask his contempt.

Judge Fogel spoke once more in his deep baritone. "If you have more pressing matters, perhaps you will find your way from the courtroom," he said, with only a thin veil of politeness.

The younger farmer looked suddenly embarrassed and tucked his head shamefully. His lips mouthed the words "Sorry," as if unable to speak them aloud. To his right, the wiry-haired farmer bore a look of disgust on his face like an ugly scar. It was plain to all present that he wasn't keen taking orders from a sheep.

Judge Fogel's black eyes set on him, unblinking, and seemed to bore deep within older man, daring him to defy the command. The gaze pressed into the man's soul until he could take it no longer and looked down at his lap, clasping his hands nervously. Judge Fogel's eyes lingered for a moment longer as if subconsciously pushing the man's will far beneath the surface. When the old sheep finally released his gaze, the audience seemed to exhale as one, once more able to breathe through the tension.

Judge Fogel glanced toward Tibbitts. "Good morning, Mister Tibbitts," he said, the cordiality belying the moment just before.

Tibbitts stood upright on his chair. His lush chest feathers seemed to bristle and straighten, drawing focus to his mottled auburn and white breast. At his rear, his turquoise-blue tail feathers trembled and ruffled dramatically for the gallery to admire.

"Judge Fogel, it is a pleasure to see you to-day," crowed Tibbitts in the high-pitched flair of a Southern gentleman. Across the aisle, Cyrus' eyes drew to vicious slits as he looked on at Tibbitts with pure disdain. Judge Fogel nodded thought-fully at Tibbitts and then turned toward Cyrus.

"Mister Sutton, is it today?" said Judge Fogel to Cyrus. The old cat seemed to bristle at the name. For most of his life, he had simply been "Boots," the old farm cat. Yet, these proceedings somehow demanded something more formal than his com-mon name. After the emancipation, some of the animals, like Tibbitts, had opulently crowned themselves with surnames, either owing to their new place in society or simply to deride the hu-mans further. Either way, Cyrus knew well that the courtroom was no place for a name like "Boots."

"Yes, your honor," he said, somewhat reluc-tantly, not having fully embraced the name. "Cy-rus Sutton on behalf of the defendant, your honor." Behind him, the farmers twisted uneasily in their seat, clearly uncomfortable with the feline representation.

Judge Fogel nodded formally at Cyrus. "Good morning, sir."

Cyrus settled back into his chair. "Good morning, your honor. It's nice to see you," he added, the last words sliding bitterly over his coarse tongue. Judge Fogel lingered on Cyrus for a moment, as if he sensed the cat's distrust, then looked down before him at a small stack of papers the old bailiff dog had splayed across his bench after dropping them from his mammoth jaws.

"Are we ready for the defendant?" asked Judge Fogel, his eyes still peering down at the papers. One corner of the pile was marked with the dog's slobber.

"Yes, your honor," said Tibbitts, his voice oozing with deference and formality.

"Yes, we are, your honor," said Cyrus. "If I may," he started, clearing his throat, "have a moment with Mister Willis when he arrives, we would be grateful."

Judge Fogel looked thoughtfully at Cyrus for a brief second. "Of course." Then he turned slightly toward the bailiff dog. "Rufus, will you retrieve Mister Willis, please?" he asked the old dog, casting only a perfunctory glance over his shoulder.

The bailiff dog turned, pushed the rear door open with his snout, and disappeared into the shadows. The crowd began to shift in their seats, the anticipation building, though none dared speak. Judge Fogel stared blankly at the back wall of the courtroom, awaiting the defendant's arrival. Tibbitts seemed to sit upright, his body rigid and firm, giving the appearance of a gamecock. Across the aisle, Cyrus paced in small, agile circles on his chair, his long, gray tail standing upright.

After several long moments, the rear door edged open, and the sound of shuffling feet could be heard in the darkened hallway. Then, a man's grim, angular face appeared from the shadows like the edge of a crescent moon. Once more, the courtroom started to buzz with hushed whispers and the rustling of feathers. The man took one hesitant step forward, then two, and emerged from the shadows, standing meekly before the courtroom in the shafts of pale sunlight that filtered through the tall windows just beside the jury box.

Dressed shabbily in a pair of dusty, faded overalls atop a rumpled, dark cotton shirt, Samuel Willis looked anything but the long-awaited centerpiece of the day's courtroom spectacle. His angular chin, covered with a thin layer of gritty, white stubble, jutted prominently below a pair of sunken eyes that divulged the truth of his soul — broken and hollow. Across the crown of his head, thin stalks of coarse white hair sprouted like a neatly trimmed lawn. Willis looked down at his feet, his eyes seeming to focus nervously on the tips of his cracked and stained leather boots. His hands were clasped before him, bound at the wrists with old iron handcuffs on a thick metal chain.

The bailiff dog pressed him forward, nosing his snout into the back of Willis' thigh. Slowly, begrudgingly, Willis stepped deeper into the courtroom, his eyes following the straight lines of the maple planks that comprised the courtroom floor. Step by step, he shuffled along, turning slightly in front of Judge Fogel's bench and maneuvering his way toward Cyrus, who had stopped circling the chair and stood stationary, watching his bedraggled client approach.

On the other side of the aisle, Tibbitts gazed straight ahead, seemingly above the humdrum moment of Willis' entry. By all appearances, Tibbitts' purpose seemed far greater than the single, shabby man who ambled past him.

With plodding steps, Willis walked slowly across the courtroom as a hush drew over the crowd. From the gallery of humans, someone spoke.

"We're with you, Sam!" barked an elderly farmer from the back row. There was a wave of muttering and heads nodding as the others consented to the words. Judge Fogel raised his wide-set eyes to the crowd but said nothing in return, electing to let the tension subside naturally.

Finally, Willis drew near Cyrus and slumped down in the hard, wooden seat beside him. He rested his cuffed hands on his lap and slouched forward. The moment weighed heavily on the old man, and he seemed to wilt at the defense table as if he longed to be anywhere but the focus of this courtroom drama.

Cyrus looked at Judge Fogel but said nothing. Judge Fogel simply nodded in return. With the subtle acknowledgement, Cyrus turned toward Willis, who leaned into him. Across the courtroom, there was silence except for the indecipherable, sibilant sounds flowing from Cyrus' mouth. Willis nodded several times. After a moment, he dipped his head closer toward Cyrus and his lips moved, asking a question. Cyrus lowered his head and pressed his mouth closer to Willis' ear and then the old farmer nodded once more.

Cyrus rested back on his haunches and studied his client for a moment, ensuring he had processed the information. Then he turned to Judge Fogel and spoke. "Thank you, your honor. We are ready to proceed."

Judge Fogel nodded, his long snout lowering slowly in formal acknowledgement. "Do we have any preliminary motions this morning, gentlecreatures?" he asked, turning first to Tibbitts.

"None from the Animals," replied Tibbitts, eager to proceed.

Judge Fogel turned once more toward Cyrus.

Cyrus lifted his head. "Your honor, we would request that the witnesses be sequestered."

Judge Fogel nodded almost imperceptibly and turned once more toward Tibbitts. "Mister Tibbitts, do the Animals have any objection?"

Tibbitts scratched at his chair with his toes. "Your honor," he said then paused, collecting his thoughts. "The Animals will not object to sequestration of the witnesses," he answered slowly, clearly choosing to pick his battles.

"Very well," replied Judge Fogel. "It is so ordered that the witnesses will be sequestered." Cyrus glanced at Willis, who looked back at him, his face a mask of perpetual uncertainty. Judge Fogel turned to the bailiff dog. "Rufus, will you please remove any witnesses from the courtroom?"

Without hesitation, the old bailiff dog strode into the center of the courtroom. "Are there any witnesses in the courtroom?" he barked.

Behind Tibbitts, an old cow rose to her feet and stood slowly, yet proudly, her eyes scanning the courtroom. In the back of the gallery, a lean, wiry dog also stood. On the humans' side of the aisle, a burly farmer with broad shoulders and a thick, dark beard stood as well. The bailiff dog scanned the room, looking at the cow, the dog, and the man. "Is there anyone else?"

Near the door, the old donkey stood slowly on achy joints. The Holsteins around him shuffled to the side to give him space. He took one long, slow step toward the door and then another. His legs creaked like the wooden benches that surrounded him.

The bailiff dog looked around. No others stood. "The witnesses will leave the courtroom and shall remain in the hallway until you are called." Then he stepped forward and pressed open the short swinging doors that separated the well of the courtroom from the gallery. "Follow me," he added, leading the way to the tall set of double doors at the rear of the courtroom that led to the hallway.

The burly farmer stepped out into the aisle first, ensuring his place before the animals. As he walked, he passed the lanky dog, quivering beside the back row, and the man's knee brushed roughly against the dog, who jerked backward in fear. The Holstein stepped from her row, her hooves clunking on the wooden floor, and followed the bailiff dog and the man out the doors into the hallway. As the enormous cow passed, the lanky dog stepped in quickly behind her, glancing nervously around the courtroom, keenly aware of the dozens of eyes upon him. The donkey stood patiently, allowing others to pass. It was clear he would be the slowest, and when the procession entered the hallway, he hobbled after them.

A murmur drew over the courtroom as the occupants muttered and buzzed. At his table, Tibbitts turned back to his papers, continuously shuffling them with his beak as if digging for insects. Across the aisle, Cyrus conferred with Willis, their words lost in the din of the crowd. At his bench, Judge Fogel stared silently at the door, waiting patiently for the bailiff dog to return.

After several long moments, the double wooden doors swung open, and the bailiff dog returned, striding confidently down the hallway and pushing open the small swinging doors.

"Gentlecreatures," said Judge Fogel once the bailiff dog was settled back over his right shoulder. Tibbitts looked up from the papers. Judge Fogel waited a moment while Cyrus finished conversing with Willis.

When the cat was finished, he turned toward Judge Fogel and spoke. "I apologize, your honor."

Judge Fogel nodded rigidly. "Are we ready for the jury?"

Tibbitts raised his beak high and puffed his chest regally as if preparing to announce the arrival of dawn. "The Animals are ready, your honor."

Judge Fogel turned to Cyrus.

"The Defense is also ready, your honor."

Then, Judge Fogel turned and nodded to the bailiff dog, who had already pushed through door into the dark hallway beyond the courtroom. The dog was gone for a moment and then returned, pushing the door open and holding it wide with his hindquarters.

A cacophonous shuffling of claws and hooves arose from the darkness of the hallway. In the gallery, the humans and animals leaned forward on the edge of their benches. The courtroom buzzed with a palpable sense that the formalities had ended and the substance of the day was soon to begin.

From the hallway, the jury slowly emerged, one by one. A bald-headed turkey led the procession, his eyes wide and his long, pink neck swaying forward and back as he stepped anxiously into the courtroom. Behind him, a tawny brown goat stumbled clumsily, quickening his pace to follow the turkey around the railing toward the rows of wooden chairs. Behind them followed the rest of the jury: two dingy white chickens; a wide, waddling pig, her pink skin covered with thick white fur and mottled with black spots; a snow white duck shuffling comically on his wide, webbed feet; and a stern-looking, Suffolk sheep whose shiny eyes set against his jet-black face glimmered dramatically in the electric lights of the courtroom. The awkward group ambled along the white wooden rail edging the jury box and stepped up the single wooden step, one by one, taking their seats with a flutter of wings and a clatter of hooves.

When they were seated on their haunches or nesting comfortably on the chairs, Judge Fogel turned to them and spoke. His voice was low and somber, and the courtroom observed in rapt attention. "Members of the jury, your solemn duty here today is to decide whether the defendant, Samuel Willis, is guilty of the crime of murder only upon the facts and evidence provided in this case." Judge Fogel paused for a moment, his deep black eyes studying the members of the jury.

Willis stiffened in his chair. A frown creased his face. The man looked defeated before the trial had begun. Sensing this, Cyrus turned to him and his eyes narrowed, summoning the fight within the old farmer. Willis' features seemed to tighten, his resolve fortified by the determination of his counsel. He nodded resolutely at the cat.

"The prosecution, Mister Tibbitts," Judge Fogel nodded at the rooster standing at attention, "bears the burden of proving the Defendant's guilt beyond a reasonable doubt."

The goat shifted nervously in his seat in the jury box.

"This burden remains with Mister Tibbitts throughout the trial," said Judge Fogel, his eyes still affixed on the jury.

Tibbitts' small, beady eyes scanned the jury, examining their faces for any helpful insight from their expressions. The turkey stared straight ahead at Judge Fogel, his face unreadable. Beside him, the two chickens bobbed their heads slightly, fully immersed in the judge's instructions. Nearby, the sheep's eyes swept across the audience in the gallery, silently absorbing the bustling crowd of farmers and workmen.

"Members of the jury, please raise your respective appendages and repeat after me," commanded Judge Fogel. In the jury box, the jurors obediently lifted their hooves and wings, holding them high in the air.

Judge Fogel raised his right hoof. "I do solemnly swear and affirm that I will conscientiously try the charges against the Defendant and will decide them only according to the evidence presented here today."

The humans in the gallery stirred and mumbled, their disgruntled voices seeping insidiously across the courtroom.

"The gallery will be quiet," barked the bailiff dog. Judge Fogel's eyes shifted to the gallery, but he never turned his head. Then his gaze returned to the jury, and he nodded.

"I do," they said in a chorus of squawks, bellows, and chirps.

Judge Fogel continued, "You may put your appendages down." He looked down at the papers on his bench for a moment and then lifted his head once more to the jury. "Members of the jury, the Defendant, Samuel Willis, duly residing in the town of Plum Grove, is before this court today, charged with one count of murder in the death of Miss Ofelia, a dairy cow formerly owned by the Defendant."

There was a sudden buzz through the crowd as the charges were read. Judge Fogel pressed onward. "If found guilty of this charge, he may be punished," he paused for a moment but never looked up, "with death by hanging from the gallows until such time as he is pronounced dead." The magnitude of the words drew a blanket of hushed silence over the courtroom.

Samuel Willis dropped his chin to his chest. Across the aisle, Tibbitts subconsciously scratched at the seat of his chair.

"Prosecutor, are you ready to proceed?" asked

Judge Fogel, turning his head slightly toward Tibbitts.

Tibbitts rose proudly in his chair and nodded. "The Animals are ready, your Honor."

Judge Fogel turned toward Cyrus. "Defense counsel, are you ready?"

"The Defense is ready, your Honor." Cyrus' yellow eyes seemed to sparkle with grim determination.

"Mister Tibbitts, you may begin," said Judge Fogel.

CHAPTER 2

The shrill creaking of the tall-backed chair pierced the silence of the courtroom as Judge Fogel leaned back and adjusted himself, settling in for the openings. A dour look fell over Willis's face, and he lifted his head slightly and gazed behind Cyrus toward Tibbitts, who stood on his chair, glancing down at his papers.

After a moment, Tibbitts hopped down to the floor and stepped forward into the well of the courtroom, his toes clicking on the wood. As one, the spectators —humans and animals alike — leaned forward on the edge of the benches, hoping to catch a glimpse of the illustrious rooster.

Those fortunate enough to see over the bannister and beyond the tables sat enraptured at the bird. He stepped slowly and methodically, his long toes stretching carefully across the thin wooden planks in measured paces. His coal-black eyes stared thoughtfully at the floor as he paced theatrically toward the jury box.

The courtroom was still except for the faint, impatient tapping of Cyrus' claws on the edge of the wooden table.

"Members of the jury," said Tibbitts, slowly raising his head to meet their eyes.

He scanned slowly left and right among them and then continued, his voice soft yet poignant. "Today, you are tasked with a most important duty." The crowd leaned forward into his words.

"Among the vast numbers of creatures on man's farms and in his factories," his eyes fixed on each of jury for a brief second as he spoke, "you have been chosen to bear the burden of judgment today."

In the jury box, one of the shabby chickens looked nervous; her head bobbed, and her feathers seemed to tremble. On the chicken's right, the Suffolk sheep stared at Tibbitts intently, his gaze solemn.

"Make no mistake; today is no ordinary day, gentlecreatures," continued Tibbitts. "Today is the day that this *man*," he said, the word punctuated with harshness as he spread his right wing wide and pointed at Willis, "will be judged for his deeds."

Willis adjusted in his seat uncomfortably and looked down at the table. From the humans seated in the gallery behind him, a faint murmur arose.

"Members of the jury, today the prosecution will show beyond a reasonable doubt that Samuel Willis, in a cold and calculating manner, brutally killed Miss Ofelia." Tibbitts paced to the far end of the jury box, where the sheep and the duck sat attentively. He leaned his beak beneath the rail and spoke, his tone softening.

"Tired and worn from years of milking, Ofelia was worth nothing to him," he said directly to the duck, his inflection rising as if matter-of-factly discussing the matter with a friend. The duck sat engrossed.

"Today, you will learn that the defendant, Samuel Willis, ran a dairy just west of the town of Plum Grove. For thirty years, he churned out gallon after gallon of milk from a herd of almost one hundred cows who lived enslaved, like the victim, at his farm."

Tibbitts broke his gaze from the duck and began to stride down the length of the bannister before the jury box. "Samuel Willis lived his life on the back of his cows. His milk filled the bellies of students at Plum Grove Elementary School. It lined the shelves at the general stores from here to Hargrove Bluff."

When he reached the edge of the jury box, Tibbitts swiveled around and paced back in the other direction, his eyes affixed to the ground. "For

Samuel Willis, milk meant everything. The cows who lived in his squalid pastures provided for him. But when they stopped providing, they were worthless." He spat these last words, his tone harsh and aggressive.

"And when Ofelia went to the ground in the dairy barn just beyond the milking parlor, *she* was worthless to Samuel Willis." He paused for a long moment, allowing silence to settle over the courtroom.

"And once he realized she was worthless, there was nothing left to do but dispose of her." Without warning, Tibbitts opened his right wing and slammed it hard on the wooden railing of the bannister. "Wham!" he squawked as he slammed the wing hard into the wood. The jurors startled and lurched back in their seats.

"One fatal blow from the blunt end of an axe to Ofelia's skull," Tibbitts said, his voice growing quiet again. He stepped back from the railing, giving the jurors reprieve. "One fatal blow of cold, hard steel crashing into the top of her skull."

Tibbitts turned, slowly paced away from the jury box, and stood in the center of the courtroom, looking out toward the gallery. "That was her reward," he said softly and lowered his eyes to the floor once more.

"For five years, Ofelia served Samuel Willis

diligently, providing him the milk he demanded. And when she could provide no more, he reined hard steel into her skull while she lay suffering on the ground." Tibbitts clasped his wings behind his back thoughtfully and paced back to the jury box.

"Members of the jury, the Animals will prove today, beyond a reasonable doubt, that Samuel Willis brutally killed Ofelia while she lay helpless in that barn."

He stepped to his left where the two chickens sat enraptured. "You will hear from the last animal to see Ofelia alive. She will tell you that Ofelia was injured, helpless on the floor of the barn. She will tell you that Ofelia was alive when all the other animals had passed and that the victim pleaded with her to help — pleaded with her because *she knew,*" he squawked the last words for emphasis and then repeated them, "*she knew* what it meant to be down on the ground. It meant that she was no good for Willis anymore and he was going to kill her." The crowd whispered.

"But that isn't all, members of the jury. Today, you will hear from an eyewitness who saw Willis enter the barn where the ailing victim lay helpless. This witness will tell you how he heard that dull thud and how Willis, only moments later, exited the barn and wiped blood from the axe on the tall weeds of the pasture."

Tibbitts paced back toward the center of the courtroom, allowing the jury to marinate in the words. Then, after a short silence, he paced back and stood before them.

"Finally, members of the jury, you will hear from a witness who will tell you that, on the following day, Willis threatened him if he didn't pull the plow. Willis told him," Tibbitts raised his wings in the air as if indicating quotations marks, "that he had better pull that plow or he would suffer the same fate as the old heifer."

Once more, Tibbitts strode the length of the jury box, his eyes scanning the back row. "Members of the jury, you will hear from these witnesses how the defendant murdered Ofelia. The animals who lived and worked on that farm will tell you what they heard and what they saw. They will tell you that Ofelia was alive when all the animals had passed. They will tell you that the defendant entered the barn where Ofelia lay helpless and alone. They will tell you of the dull thud and the sounds of metal crashing into her skull. They will tell you that the defendant emerged from that barn and wiped blood from the axe. And they will tell you that the defendant threatened them with the *very same thing* he did to Ofelia."

Judge Fogel shifted slightly in his chair, pushing unnaturally at the bunches in his robe with his hoof.

"Members of the jury, in response to this evidence against him, the defendant will tell you that it didn't happen that way. He will tell you not to believe the last animal to see Ofelia alive. He will tell you not to believe his own, loyal dog, who saw him wipe blood from the axe. He will tell you that the donkey he threatened is old and senile and can't remember what Willis said." Tibbitts stood square in the center of the railing before the jury, seeming to absorb them all as one with his intense gaze.

"He will tell you to forget everything, to discard every bit of common sense, to forgo all logic and reason, and believe that this farmer, this kind, benevolent farmer," he said with a look of contempt, "would never do such a thing to his prized cows — to his *family*, as they will undoubtedly say."

Tibbitts turned and walked slowly back toward his chair at the prosecution table, signaling he had nearly concluded. As he reached the table, he turned and looked at the jury once more. "But you know better than that. You know the animals of Samuel Willis' farm are far from his family. You know that Ofelia and the others just like her were machines — pieces of property for Samuel Willis to use and exploit for his precious dollars."

He cast his eyes to the tall window just to the left of the jury box, looking longingly into the crisp Plum Grove morning. "And you will soon know that, in that dingy milking barn, as Ofelia lay broken and helpless on the ground, having served Samuel Willis until her body simply gave out, he raised that axe high above her. Her eyes grew wide in terror as she stared up at him, and in the glow of the single lantern, that steel blade came crashing into her skull, one final indignity laid upon her by Samuel Willis."

"*This*," he drew out the word, "members of the jury, is what the Animals will prove here today. And we ask you to find the defendant guilty of murder in the death of Ofelia."

With his final words, Tibbitts strode the last few paces behind his table. Cyrus' eyes drew to slits as the rooster passed beside him. Tibbitts crouched and hopped in one sudden motion, fluttering his wings briefly. As he landed in his chair, he tucked his feathers, turned to Judge Fogel, and nodded, affirming that he was finished.

Judge Fogel leaned forward in his chair and looked to Cyrus. "Mister Sutton, are you ready?" he asked.

Without a word, Cyrus jumped down from his chair silently, his long, gray tail arced in the air as he paced toward the jury. As he passed Judge

Fogel's bench, he turned and said, "Yes, your honor," then continued toward the jury box.

The cat's whiskers rippled, and his broad face looked resolute. At the defense table, Willis leaned forward in his chair, and the faintest glimmer of hope creased his troubled face.

"Nonsense," said Cyrus simply as he reached the bannister and stopped. For a long moment, he stood there in the silence of the courtroom, scanning the eyes of the jury.

"The Animals will have you believe *nonsense*," he added, the word curt and harsh. "We gather here today at a profound moment in our history. The animals of the fields and barns have been liberated —emancipated," he said, seeming to settle on the proper word.

"For decades, the animals toiled on farms and in factories, but now, you are free. Yet, there are some among you who seek vengeance — retribution for the past." Without subtlety, he cast his gaze toward Tibbitts.

"Mister Tibbitts will have you believe that what happened to the victim is a violent act by a violent man. He will have you believe that Samuel Willis, outraged and angered at her failure to stand, beat her to death with the back end of an axe." Cyrus began to slink down the length of the jury box.

"But the reality of what happened in that milking barn just before the great emancipation is hardly so interesting." When he reached the end of the jury box, he stopped just before the turkey and the brown goat and peered up at them through the rails.

"The Defense concedes that Ofelia was down on the ground, unable to rise. But contrary to what Mister Tibbitts will have you believe, she was not killed by a blow from an axe." Cyrus stood silently for a moment before continuing.

"Far from the salacious story Mister Tibbitts will tell you today, Ofelia was, in fact, trampled by a careless cow passing through the barn after milking. Her skull was crushed by the hooves of someone who Mister Tibbitts will conveniently sit before you as his star witness. She'll tell you how she saw Ofelia on the ground of the milking barn, how Ofelia pleaded with her for help."

In the gallery, the farmers leaned forward on their benches, attuned to Cyrus' words. Judge Fogel's beady eyes shifted at the movement and then returned to the cat.

"But if Ofelia indeed pleaded for help, it was because the Animals' star witness had trampled her, stepped on her head, and smashed her skull, an injury that would ultimately lead to her death. So, when you hear Mister Tibbitts' star witness, ask yourself — does this sound like the words of someone seeking to shirk blame for actually killing Ofelia?"

"Members of the jury, the great emancipation was undoubtedly long overdue," the words seemed to sour on his tongue, "but today is not the day to judge this fact." Cyrus pivoted nimbly and glided down the length of the jury box. "Nor is today the day to seek vengeance for the victim," he added, his words rising into a throaty howl.

When he reached the far end of the jury box, just before the sheep who stared transfixed at the slinking cat, he stopped and his eyes scanned the length of the jury once more. "Today is the day for truth," he declared profoundly, his yellowish eyes settling on each one of the seven jurors. In the back row, the brown goat shifted in his seat when the eyes fell upon him. Beside him, the mottled pig sat slack-jawed at rapt attention, a faint strand of drool running from the corner of her mouth.

Cyrus continued, "As we sift through the obfuscations put forth today by Mister Tibbitts, the truth will become quite clear. You will see that Samuel Willis was a decent, honorable farmer. For years, he cared for cows just like Ofelia and goats and fowl just like many of you." The two chickens seemed to bristle at the word.

"Each morning before the sun rose, Samuel

Willis rose and toiled in the fields and in the barns to provide for the scores of animals who called his farm home. Samuel Willis is a noble, decent man. Yet today, the Animals seek to use him as a scapegoat for sins of the past." The brown goat's eyes drew to slits, and he glowered at Cyrus, who seemed to realize his mistake much too late.

"Mister Tibbitts seeks to use Mister Willis as an *excuse*," he corrected himself awkwardly.

"Members of the jury, the truth will speak to you today if you allow it. If you cast aside the shroud of bloodlust that Mister Tibbitts attempts to cast over your deliberations, the truth is right before you." He extended his right arm symbolically, paw upward. "And the truth is that Samuel Willis did not kill Ofelia. *That*, members of the jury, is the only truth today."

And with that, Cyrus's eyes panned the jury once more then he turned gracefully and walked back to the defense table, springing effortlessly into the wooden chair. Willis leaned over and whispered a few words to the cat and nodded appreciatively.

Judge Fogel leaned forward in his chair, his deep black eyes watching Cyrus carefully until he settled in his chair. Then, he looked over to Tibbitts. "Mister Tibbitts, you may call your first witness."

CHAPTER 3

As the towering oak doors in the rear of the courtroom creaked and opened slightly, the gallery turned as one in their seats. For a brief second, the doors gaped and revealed only the timeworn turquoise and white checkered tile of the courthouse hallway. Then, a long shadow loomed in the opening, preceding the shape of a large, black and white Holstein cow. Once more, a subdued murmur rose within the courtroom.

The cow, Geraldine, entered the courtroom slowly, her eyes shifting nervously from left to right between the animals on one side and the glum, disapproving faces of the humans on the other. On her lean, bony legs, she stepped slowly down the aisle, her sharp, protruding pelvis bones rising and falling at her cadence.

To her right, the humans' faces furrowed and scowled as looks of abhorrence cast upon her like an icy sleet. The old cow looked down with her thoughtful eyes as she walked and pressed forward, pushing her nose into the low, double doors that swung open before her.

Judge Fogel lowered his head to examine her carefully, as if he were peering over a pair of non-existent spectacles. As she passed the tables, Willis raised his head and glanced toward her; an instinctual flash of disgust crossed his face. Beside him, Cyrus sat calmly, his slate-gray tail whisking back and forth across the vertical wooden rods on the back of his chair.

Geraldine moved gingerly to the witness box, her hooves clonking on the tile as she pulled her gaunt frame along with determined steps. She placed her two front hooves up into the witness box and pushed the wooden chair aside with her nose. The shrill sliding of the wooden legs across the tile echoed through the courtroom. Then, she stepped carefully into the witness box and positioned herself facing the audience. With a huff and a grunt of her tired joints, she rested back on her haunches, her angular head visible several feet above the small table before her.

Judge Fogel cleared his throat softly, and Geraldine turned slightly toward him. "Miss Geraldine, do you swear to tell the truth, the whole truth, and nothing but the truth?"

Geraldine answered without hesitation. "I do."

Judge Fogel nodded then turned from Geraldine to Tibbitts, lowering his head and looking down his narrow snout. "Mister Tibbitts," he said, the statement sounding like a question.

"Yes, your honor," said Tibbitts as he hopped swiftly down from his chair and stepped with long, careful strides into the well of the courtroom. "Good morning, Miss Geraldine."

"Good morning," said Geraldine, her voice soft but clear. The words were carefully articulated and carried with them an unmistakable pain.

"Will you please state your name for the jury?" said Tibbitts.

Geraldine looked at Tibbitts, digesting the question, and then as if prompted by him, shifted her body toward the jury. The seven animals looked back at her.

"My name is Geraldine."

"And Miss Geraldine, will you please tell us what your, uh—" Tibbitts seemed to fumble theatrically with the words, "—what your *former* job was?" he said, his pitch rising with the word. A wave of whispers rose among the crowd.

Judge Fogel interjected instantly. "The audience will be silent," he commanded. Without effort, his voice boomed over the heads of the attorneys and soaked into the denizens of the gallery. The ripple of sound from the crowd subsided before he had finished his words.

Geraldine shifted in the witness box. "I was a . . . a dairy cow . . . for Farmer Willis," she said, the words incongruous with the understated sophistication of her tone. She lifted her gaze and cast it dispassionately toward her former master. Willis' lip curled upward in a malignant scowl.

"Now, Miss Geraldine, I want to talk about why we're here today," said Tibbitts, allowing just enough time for her statement to linger in the air before proceeding. "Did you know the victim, Miss Ofelia?"

Geraldine nodded.

"Please speak your answers, ma'am," interrupted Judge Fogel.

"Yes, sir," said Geraldine, still instinctively nodding. "I knew Ofelia."

"And how did you know Ofelia?"

"She was one of the herd."

Tibbitts took two long steps toward Geraldine, his head bowed and his wings twisted thoughtfully behind his back. "By herd, you mean the dairy herd, correct?"

Geraldine nodded again and then caught herself. "Yes, yes, that's what I mean."

"And how long did you know Ofelia?"

"I knew her for her whole life."

Tibbitts lifted his head and looked at her as if

urging her to say more. She seemed to notice and continued.

"Ofelia was born on the farm several years ago. Her mother worked with me, and then—" Geraldine paused thoughtfully for a brief second, "—Ofelia did, too."

Tibbitts turned and walked toward the jury. "Miss Geraldine, how old would you say Ofelia was?" he said as he positioned himself carefully in the line of sight between the witness and jury.

She lifted her gaze from the floor and looked up at Tibbitts. "She was probably four years old."

"And was she in good health?" asked the rooster.

Cyrus rose from his seat. "Objec—"

"No, no she wasn't," said Geraldine before the cat could finish.

"—tion!" rasped Cyrus, pressing the word out with urgency. "Objection, your honor!" he clamored, a hint of exasperation barely concealed in his tone.

Without turning in his seat, Judge Fogel's eyes swiveled and looked down at Cyrus.

Cyrus gathered himself for a moment. "Your honor, this witness has not been qualified as an expert veterinarian and is in no position to comment on the relative health of the victim."

Judge Fogel's eyes swiveled to Tibbitts. "Sustained," he said flatly without allowing a rebuttal. "The witness may comment only on her observations, but she may not speculate on any medical conditions."

Tibbitts continued unfazed. "Miss Geraldine, will you please explain to the jury — in great detail," he said, seeming to take some delight in the words, "your personal observations about the victim's physical condition?" Tibbitts turned and cast a brief glance at Cyrus, whose tail swished rapidly in long, circular strokes.

"Ofelia did not look well," she said somewhat vaguely.

Tibbitts lowered his head and looked up at her, waiting for her to continue. "She had been ill for a long time prior to her death . . . frothing at the mouth, limping. She didn't sleep well, and her stool . . . was well, she was having problems, you might say."

Tibbitts stood motionless by the jury box, allowing her to continue.

"For several weeks before she died, she was getting weaker and weaker. She didn't want to go to the milking barn. She said it wore her down."

Cyrus shot upright on his chair on all fours. "Objection, hearsay!"

"Objection sustained," said Judge Fogel languidly without looking in the cat's direction.

"Miss Geraldine, you may not repeat what anyone told you. You must only state your own personal observations. Do you understand?"

Geraldine looked at him and nodded apologetically.

"You may continue," said Judge Fogel.

"She would get tired very easily. The milking took a lot out of her. Each time they took her babies away . . . it took a lot out of her. Her body was . . . well . . . her body was failing her, and we all knew what would happen when she couldn't produce milk anymore."

Cyrus pivoted sharply in his chair and glowered at Tibbitts, almost challenging Tibbitts to ask the question.

Tibbitts knew better. "Miss Geraldine, did you see Ofelia on the day she was killed?"

Willis whispered to Cyrus, who leaned into his ear and offered a few words in return.

"I did," said Geraldine somberly.

"Will you please talk the jury through the last time you saw Geraldine?" asked Tibbitts.

"We were in the milking parlor together — me, Geraldine, and eight other cows."

Tibbitts nodded for her to continue.

"Farmer Willis had just finished milking us. We were headed back through the barn to the pasture as we always did."

"Miss Geraldine, let me stop you right there," interrupted Tibbitts. "When you say you were headed through the barn, this is a barn the herd is moved through on the way to the milking parlor, is that correct?"

"Yes. Farmer Willis takes ten cows at a time into the milking parlor. That's how many will fit in the stalls. To get to the parlor, we have to pass through the old red barn."

"And will you please describe the barn?"

Geraldine shifted uncomfortably on her knobby haunches. "It is not much of a barn — made of dark red wood — rather old. There are stalls along the right side as you enter, filled with old, moldy straw. Sometimes, if a cow gets sick while milking, Farmer Willis will—" she paused, "—move her to one of the stalls to get her out of the way."

"When you say *move*," said Tibbitts, emphasizing the word, "what do you mean?"

Cyrus rose once more in his chair. "Your honor," he said, this time taking a polite approach as if realizing sustained brashness might grind on Judge Fogel. "I do not see the relevance of the question."

"Your honor, I withdraw the question," said Tibbitts without prompting, looking coy.

Judge Fogel simply nodded.

"Miss Geraldine, will you tell us exactly what happened on the day in question?"

Geraldine looked down somberly at the wooden railing before her as if gathering her thoughts. "Ofelia had not been feeling well for quite some time. The humans call it 'milk fever'."

Tibbitts interjected. "Will you tell the jury what you mean by 'milk fever'?"

Geraldine's gaze seemed to wander to the tall ten-pane windows on the far side of the jury box. "Cows get sick at the farm a lot. Sometimes, they've been worked too hard and just can't work anymore. Sometimes, they're sick. Could be lots of things — a birth took a lot out of them, cold from the weather, sick from the food, or maybe just something wrong inside their body. Farmer Willis, well, whatever it was, he would always call it 'milk fever'."

Willis shifted angrily in his chair. His eyes seemed to bore into Geraldine, yet she continued staring out through the tall windows. Wispy white clouds glided across the sunlit sky beyond the panes of dusty glass.

"So, you're saying that 'milk fever' is sort of a general term for a lot of things wrong with the cows?" asked Tibbitts.

"Yes."

"And Ofelia had what you call 'milk fever'?"

"*He* called it 'milk fever'," said Geraldine, finally breaking her gaze from the window and nodding toward Willis.

Cyrus looked like he may object but allowed it to continue.

"He always called it 'milk fever'," said Geraldine.

"Now, please continue and tell the jury what happened that day," prodded Tibbitts.

"As I said, Ofelia wasn't feeling well for a long time. She was having chills, wasn't eating much, and her legs were weak. That day, we were all in the milking stalls, lined up one by one like always. Ofelia was in the stall next to me."

"On your left or right?" asked Tibbitts, gesturing respectively with each wing in turn.

"She was on my left. I was in the furthest stall by the wall. She was one over." She paused for a moment and then, without prompting, continued. "I knew that she wasn't feeling well. She looked like she might fall over." At the words, the Holsteins in the gallery seemed to grow visibly uneasy.

"And how did you know this? Did you notice any outward signs that she was weak or not feeling well?"

"Yes, you could see that her legs were wobbly. The whole way up the hill in the pasture, she lagged behind the others, so I waited for her. I stood there and watched her and knew she was going to go down."

Judge Fogel turned his head slowly, scanning the courtroom as she spoke. The audience sat in hushed silence.

"What happened next?" said Tibbitts.

"Farmer Willis came in and started attaching the milking tubes to all of us. He started at the far end, away from me. When he got to Ofelia, he could tell she wasn't doing well. She was wobbling in her stall like she might fall at any minute."

Geraldine paused again as if collecting her thoughts. "He got down on his knees and put the first tubes on, and she swayed to her left like she was going to fall. Farmer Willis jumped to his feet from under her and stood up quickly."

The audience shifted in their seats as if something noteworthy was coming. Tibbitts sensed the anticipation and prodded Geraldine along. "And then?" he said, leading her.

"He shouted at her, cursed and yelled at her for almost falling over on him."

Tibbitts took a few paces backward down the rail of the jury box, ensuring he was not obstructing the jury's view of the witness stand. Her eyes followed him down the length of the jury as he moved.

Then she continued, "He wound up his arm and punched her hard in the side."

Once more, the crowd began to murmur, and Willis shifted, seemingly unable to find comfort in his wooden chair.

Tibbitts stood silently at the far end of the jury box, his wings folded behind his back.

"She let out a loud noise like the wind came out of her. I saw her wobble again and lean against the railing. Then he came into her stall and took her halter and yanked it backward and started tugging her out of the stall."

"Did she come out of the stall?" asked Tibbitts softly.

"She did," she replied. "He practically dragged her out and then led her down the aisle into the barn. I turned my head and watched her go through the door into the barn. He stopped by the first stall there on the left, and I saw his arm go back again and punch her hard in her side."

Willis leaned over toward Cyrus and whispered urgently. Cyrus' pointed ear swiveled toward Willis, and he dipped his head slightly to listen then shook his head back and forth. Willis' face drew a frown, and he slouched back in his chair.

Tibbitts glanced over quickly at the defense table and then back to Geraldine. "What did you see next?"

"I saw her legs buckle, and she slumped over sideways then fell to the ground." She turned and looked toward the defense table. "Then after a minute, Farmer Willis came back in and attached the milking equipment to me and finished milking the remaining cows."

"Could you see Ofelia from where you were?"

Geraldine's wide, dark eyes grew thoughtful. "I could see the shape of her body in the barn. It was dark in there, but I knew she was lying on the ground just outside the door."

"And when you were finished being milked, what happened?"

"Farmer Willis came and led us out of the parlor."

"Back through the barn?"

"Yes, back through the barn."

"And did you pass Ofelia on the way out?"

"We did. She was lying there on the ground — halfway in the stall, halfway in the aisle."

"So you had to walk around her?" asked Tibbitts as he took a few steps toward the center of the courtroom as if cuing the response.

"Yes, we were able to get through the door, and Farmer Willis herded us around her. There was just enough room to get around."

"What did you see when you passed her?" asked Tibbitts, turning back to Geraldine.

"She looked up at me as I passed. I could tell she was very sick. Her eyes . . . you can just tell." Geraldine stopped and looked down at the floor, seeming to compose herself. "She was hurting. She'd just been worked too hard."

Cyrus rose quickly to all fours on his chair in a flash. "Objection!" he caterwauled. "*Again*, your honor," he said in unbridled frustration, "the witness is not a veterinary expert and is in no position to comment on the cause of the victim's injuries!"

Judge Fogel turned and looked at Tibbitts, who said nothing then looked at the jury. "The jury will disregard the witness' speculation on the cause of the victim's injuries," he droned unenthusiastically.

Judge Fogel nodded at Tibbitts to continue.

"Miss Geraldine, just to be clear, Ofelia was alive when you passed her and left the barn. Is that correct?" asked Tibbitts.

"Yes, she was. She was very sick and hurting, but she was alive. He herded us out of the barn. I turned to look back, and he yanked the halter and pulled me through the door."

"And you never stepped on her by accident?"
"I did not."
"Never placed a hoof on her in any way?"
"No."
Tibbitts took several more paces to the center

of the courtroom, and his chest feathers ruffled. He dipped his beak as if deep in thought and then slowly turned to face the jury across the courtroom, drawing their gaze to him.

"What was the last thing you saw as Farmer Willis yanked your halter?"

Geraldine paused for a moment, collecting her thoughts, and the jury's eyes fell upon her as one. "I looked back at her, and in the darkness, I could see the whites of her eyes staring at me — they were almost gaping at me, like she knew the end was near."

Cyrus' legs twitched suddenly as if he were about to rise.

"No further questions, your honor," said Tibbitts before Cyrus could stand on his chair. The cat looked at him, his mouth half-agape, lodged with an unspoken objection. Then Tibbitts turned sharply on his toes and marched back to his table, flapped his wings, and nested in his chair.

The crowd stirred behind him. The humans seethed with hushed curses and coarse mutterings. Across the aisle, fur bristled and feathers ruffled.

Judge Fogel spoke, quieting the courtroom. "Mister Sutton, your witness."

Cyrus leapt from his chair without hesitation and landed silently on the wooden floor. With his long, gray tail stabbing high in the air, he stalked to the witness stand.

"Miss Geraldine," he said, the words dripping with disdain, "you said the barn was dark. Is that correct?"

"Yes, it was somewhat dark," she replied.

"You said you were in the furthest stall by the wall?" Cyrus slinked closer to the witness box.

"I was," replied Geraldine, somewhat hesitantly.

"And from that stall to the door to the barn is about forty feet?"

"I . . . I don't know how far it is."

Cyrus circled toward the jury box and then back toward the center of the courtroom. "How many cows fit in the milking parlor, Miss Geraldine?" he said, his pitch rising.

"Ten," she said softly, a hint of nervousness creeping into her voice.

"And how wide is each stall?"

"I . . . I don't really know," she said.

Cyrus turned and paced back toward the jury box. "Wide enough to fit a full grown cow?"

"Why yes, of course."

"And as you sit there in the witness box, you don't have a lot of room up there, do you?"

Geraldine shifted uncomfortably on her haunches. "No, I don't."

"So at least *ten* times the width of this witness box, wouldn't you say?"

Geraldine glanced out toward Tibbitts, who looked back at her emotionless. "Yes, that would be correct," she answered after a moment.

Cyrus pressed on with the questions. "Now, your head was tethered to the railing, was it not?"

"Yes, it was."

"So you couldn't turn your head completely sideways," Cyrus stated.

"That is correct," replied Geraldine hesitantly.

"So, with your head tethered to the railing so you couldn't even turn it sideways," he said, his voice growing stronger until it boomed across the small courtroom, "and from the length of at least ten jury boxes away, you could somehow see crystal clearly into a darkened barn. Is that what you are telling this jury today, Miss Geraldine?" His words were bitter.

In the gallery, the humans grumbled in assent.

Geraldine shifted in her seat and looked once more at Tibbitts, who only nodded back stoically. "I did not say I could see everything," she replied firmly, "but I know what I saw."

"You *know* what you saw," said Cyrus, mockingly. "You *know* what you saw," he scoffed, this time toward the gallery of humans.

Geraldine only stared down at the cat, unamused

by his antics.

After a moment, Cyrus turned and paced toward the witness stand once more then turned and leered at Geraldine. "And you claim that you were the last one out of the milking parlor?"

"That is correct," said Geraldine without hesitation.

"You were the last one to see Ofelia alive," said Cyrus, stepping closer to the witness box and starting to circle at her feet. Geraldine looked down uncomfortably.

"Yes."

"No one else was behind you?"

"That's right," said Geraldine, a subtle hint of frustration creeping into her voice.

"You said that Ofelia was halfway in the aisle?"

"She was."

"And you had to *step around her* to get by," he said, emphasizing the words.

Geraldine nodded.

"You said there was just room to get around her?"

"There was."

Cyrus' fur seemed to ripple, and he paced back to the center of the courtroom, letting the questions sink in to the jury. Then he strode silently back and sat by the end of the railing of the jury box, just near the goat whose eyes darted back and forth nervously.

"Miss Geraldine," the jury hung on his words, "you were the last one out of that barn."

Geraldine said nothing, unsure if the cat was asking a question or making a statement.

"You were the last one to see Ofelia alive?" Cyrus looked up at her; his flaxen eyes blazed with acrimony.

"You stepped on Ofelia," he said simply. The audience gasped, and Geraldine drew back in her seat, startled. "You stepped on her as you passed by in the barn."

"I did not!" retorted Geraldine.

"You didn't walk around her," he taunted.

"I did!" she bellowed.

"You went to pass her in that narrow aisle, and your clumsy hoof came down on her head, didn't it?"

"No, no, it did not," blustered Geraldine.

"And your full weight came down onto her and crushed her skull," he accused, jabbing his paw at her.

"No!"

"And you *knew* . . . you *knew* what you had done, so you concocted this whole story about Samuel Willis punching her," he continued. "In the darkness . . . with your head tied . . . from fifty feet away . . . you somehow saw Samuel Willis punching Ofelia!" howled Cyrus.

Geraldine's eyes were wide with shock. "I did no such thing!"

"You conjured this whole story because you — you're the one who killed her, aren't you?" he said, as he pressed closer to her. Geraldine sat there flummoxed, unable to speak. "You slipped in the aisle and smashed her skull. Now you see your big chance to get back at Farmer Willis. Isn't that right, Miss Geraldine?" Cyrus sneered and bared his teeth at her.

Moisture pooled in the corner of Geraldine's luminescent black eyes and rolled down her angular cheek. "I did not step on her!" she yelled back at him angrily.

Cyrus said nothing, allowing her anger to linger before the jury. Behind him, the whole audience buzzed in the gallery. From the denizens on the balcony above, a single white feather floated lazily down and landed silently on the knee of an old farmer seated below.

"No further questions, your honor." Cyrus twisted in a half-circle then slinked back to his table and effortlessly hopped into his chair beside Willis.

CHAPTER 4

After a long minute, the lingering whispers and mutters subsided, and the courtroom grew quiet once more. The bailiff dog had led Geraldine through the wide double doors as jeers and boos rained on her from her left as she hurried down the aisle as quickly as her old legs would carry her. Judge Fogel's voice boomed at the crowd for quiet, and the humans had eventually subsided. Soon, an anticipatory silence settled over the courtroom.

"Mister Tibbitts," said Judge Fogel, finally settling back in his chair. "You may call your next witness."

Tibbitts glanced over his shoulder toward the double doors, where the bailiff dog stood waiting for his command. "You may bring in Amos." The shaggy white bailiff dog nodded obediently and vanished from sight.

After a moment, the doors swung open and a ragged, skittish-looking dog entered the courtroom. Lean and wiry, his whitish coat was mottled with faint black spots and patches of chocolate brown brindle over each eye. His tongue hung out almost comically, and he panted anxiously as his eyes darted back and forth around the courtroom. The dog's fur trembled visibly as the eyes of all in the gallery fell upon the shabby creature. His quivering, unsteady form looked like it could melt at any moment and slip through the cracks in the floorboards.

The bailiff dog prodded him forward, and together, the two dogs pushed through the small double doors into the well of the courtroom. As the dog passed Cyrus, he seemed to lean away nervously from the irritable gray cat. The dog ambled hastily across the wooden floor to the witness stand and disappeared for a moment behind the table then hopped up into the chair, a natural gracefulness belying his outwardly jumpy appearance.

He sat there in the chair, staring awestruck into the gallery, his tongue flicking nervously at his lips. Then he started to pant, and his dulled, discolored teeth showed to the gallery.

"You are Amos?" asked Judge Fogel indifferently.

The dog jumped and turned at Judge Fogel, startled. His mouth closed once and then opened. "Yes, yes," he said, the words quick and erratic.

"Do you swear to tell the truth, the whole truth, and nothing but the truth?" asked Judge Fogel.

"Yes, yes," answered Amos hastily, as if the words left his mouth before he had even processed the question.

Judge Fogel nodded toward Tibbitts, who hopped down off his chair and stepped slowly toward the center of the courtroom, his long toes taking measured paces so as not to startle the dog.

"Mister Amos. Good morning," he said gently, easing the dog into the questioning.

"Good morning, good morning." Then he sat there and panted, a small bubble of saliva pooling along the corner of his mouth.

"Mister Amos, can you tell us how you know the defendant, Mister Willis?"

Amos shifted nervously in his chair, stood briefly on all fours to adjust himself, and then sat back down on his haunches, as if trying to expel the jitters from his body. He glanced quickly at Willis then looked away.

"He's my master," said the dog obediently.

Tibbitts' feathers ruffled slightly. "By master, you mean you *were* his dog. Is that right?"

"Yes," said Amos quickly, missing the significance of Tibbitt's words.

"And you lived on his farm. Is that right?"

"Yes, yes, I lived on the farm."

"Now, Mister Amos, did you have the occasion to see Mister Willis by the milking barn on the day in question?"

Amos shifted again in his chair. His eyes grew wide and nervous, and he shook his head vigorously. "Mister Amos, I'll need you to answer yes or no," urged Tibbitts.

"Yes, I did see. I saw by the barn."

"Would you please tell the jury what you saw that day?"

Amos' snout dipped low and then rose, and he swiveled his head awkwardly, scanning the jurors and then the animals in the gallery and, at last, reluctantly laying eyes on the humans gathered behind the defense table. His eyes nervously darted past Willis, avoiding eye contact. Then he gulped visibly, and his fur trembled. Around him, the deathly silence of the courtroom hung in the air like a great cloud. Over Amos' left shoulder, Judge Fogel peered over his snow-white snout down into the witness stand, his eyes boring into the dog.

And then, with the half-croaking of an animal who sounded only moments away from fainting with anxiety, Amos began to recount his story.

Far on the western horizon, the amber sun had begun its slow descent below the lonely grove of cottonwood trees, their shadowy branches cresting upward into the dusty blue sky. All around him, the tall wisps of pasture grass swayed and bent against a crisp afternoon breeze.

Just south of the milking barn, Amos trotted through the verdant fields, the blades of grass whisking away the cool stream water that clung stubbornly to his coat. This farm was his playground. As the loyal, old working dog of Farmer Willis, Amos enjoyed the run of the vast property at times like these when Farmer Willis was occupied with tasks that required the assistance of no dog.

On most days, Amos was at Farmer Willis' heels, following him from the groaning wooden steps of the old Victorian house into the fields, the coops, and the barns, heeding his commands almost before they left the old farmer's mouth. When the flock of chickens broke loose of their old wire coops, Amos was there, circling, dipping his head low, and barking at the frantic white birds to herd them back. When the sheep strayed and lollygagged in the fields, reluctant to return to their barren pasture, Amos dutifully herded them back, nipping playfully at their heels. And when the cows shuffled in their miserable line to the milking parlor, Amos followed behind, prodding them into the old red barn with yips and barks.

Now, with the downtrodden cows occupied in the milking parlor for the next several hours, there was nothing left for Amos to do. As soon as the barn doors closed, he raced across the pasture toward the wood line where the cottonwoods shielded the narrow stream that snaked through the property. Amos galloped for the stream, plunging through the small woods headlong into the cold, bubbling water. There was little he loved more than racing back and forth across the stream, splashing and snapping his jaws at the silvery shiner fish that darted beneath the clear water.

For a long time that day, Amos frolicked in the crisp, cool stream, until his mouth gaped wide and he panted, sucking in the warm summer air. Exhausted, he lay on the water's edge where the patch of cottonwoods opened just enough to let the welcome rays of sun carve through the hollow. All around him, the woodland creatures stirred. Small, russet squirrels scurried up the rough bark, and nimble, ashen-gray mockingbirds fluttered about the orchid petals of the magnolia trees. Amos lay there for a long time in bliss until the sun's rays receded through the branches and the ground grew cold in the long shadows. He stirred from his resting spot and glanced across the stream toward the farm — it was time to return to work.

He stood and trotted across the stream, stopping briefly to look at a sparkling fish that knifed past his splayed paws. Then he leapt to the bank and shook himself, large droplets soaking the leaves of the wild ferns that sprouted at the base of the cottonwoods. Satisfied he was sufficiently clean, Amos trotted through the wood line and out into the field.

Far ahead, the tall barn loomed upon the slope, the angular shape looming against the fading blue sky. To the left of the barn stood a shorter building of faded white siding, the last remnants of sun absorbed and dying in its ugly patches of rusted tin roof — the milking parlor.

Amos scanned the area for any signs of Farmer Willis. Once before, he had been late coming back from the stream, and Farmer Willis was already in the pastures with the cows. He had been none too happy at the old dog that day, and when they had gathered the cows and herded them across the field toward their corral, he had scolded Amos harshly, yelling and cursing at him. Amos had ducked his head timidly and followed alongside dutifully. When they reached the house, Farmer Willis had kicked him hard in the side, slamming his wiry body against the hard brick that ringed the base of the house. The wind expelled from Amos and he stumbled, falling there beside the doorway. He could remember the look on Farmer Willis' face — a deep, cruel scowl split his rough, stubbled chin like a hatchet mark.

"You God-damn dog," he had cursed at Amos that day. "You're lucky I need you around here or you'd be in a bag in the river," he snarled.

The words sank deep into his chest, wounding his heart as he lay there beside the house trembling. Ever since that day, he vowed that he would never again be late returning to the milking barn. As he picked up the pace and loped up the small hill, spying no movement in the pasture, he breathed a sigh of relief as he knew he was not late today.

Just as he neared the barn, its doors swung open, and the pitiful herd of old Holstein cows began to trod out, forlorn and dejected as they always were. The first two stepped into the grass of the pasture and, seeing Amos there, formed anxiously into a line. At the door, Farmer Willis stood, looking out into the field, searching for Amos. His eyes dropped and fell on the old dog, and Amos returned his look obediently, as if he had been there waiting the whole time. But Farmer Willis' nose crinkled with his perpetual disdain, and he stepped back into the shadows of the barn.

"Come on!" he grumbled at the lumbering procession of cows. Amos could hear his hand slapping them hard in their sides, and they hurried their pace into the pasture. Amos counted — one, two, three, four, five, six, seven, eight, nine. He counted again — one, two, three, four, five, six, seven, eight, nine. One was missing.

Amos circled around the cows, who were now gathered into a rough, single-file line. As he approached the doorway, he could see Farmer Willis, several paces into the barn, brushing straw and dirt out of the aisle. In the shadows, Amos saw him walk to the corner of the barn and reach for something. As the shafts of waning afternoon sun slanted through the open doorway, a dull fleck of metal shone in the shadows, and as Amos squinted his eyes, he could see that Farmer Willis had picked up an old, oak-handled axe. He turned and looked at Amos, his face shaded in the darkness.

"Get on!" he bellowed at the dog. "Move 'em back to the corral!" Amos instinctively let out a small whimper, confused by the situation. Farmer Willis approached the open barn door and jabbed his weathered hand out, grasping the wooden cross-beam and yanking it closed. For a moment, Amos stood there frozen and uncertain.

As the door squeaked drearily closed on tired, rusted hinges, the stubborn rays of sun filtered through the receding gap and pressed deeper into the barn. Through the narrowing crack, Amos could see Ofelia, splayed unceremoniously on the ground just outside the door of the milking parlor, breathing heavily. Then, the door slammed shut, and Amos stood alone in the pasture with the nine forlorn cows.

For a moment, he just stood there puzzled, and then the movement of the cows startled him as they began to stray and wander across the pasture. Not wanting to face Farmer Willis' wrath, he stirred into action, circling them and nipping at their legs until they moved in a single file toward the corral. One by one, he herded them into the corral and pushed the old wooden gate closed with his nose, listening for the tell-tale click of the latch.

As the cows dispersed glumly among the larger herd, Amos galloped back toward the milking barn, his long, wiry legs propelling him through the wisps of tall grass. Above, the faint remnants of blue sky had turned a chalky gray as the sun slipped below the tree line on the far edge of the farm.

Amos circled gracefully around the barn and headed toward the double doors, eager to plant himself outside in wait for Farmer Willis. As he rounded the front corner in haste, kicking tufts of grass into the air, a dull, sickening thud echoed from just beyond the tall red doors. An anguished moan pressed desperately through the cracks in the rotted wood, and Amos braced his legs into the soft dirt and skidded to a halt. His dark brindle ears perked, the right one standing more erect than the other as it always did, and his brow crinkled in consternation, giving the old dog a dopey appearance. He stared straight ahead and focused his senses on the other side of the door. As the tips of his mottled fur trembled, he could sense life drain away beyond the wooden walls of the barn, the echoes of its anguished cries ebbing into a cold and hollow silence. In the void, Amos' ears filled with a crisp breeze that rattled the leaves of the cottonwoods and rippled the verdant pasture. He sat there motionless, confused and frightened.

After a moment, the familiar creaking of the wooden door stirred him to life, and Farmer Willis' footsteps pounded purposefully along the hard dirt, trampled firm by the regular parades of cows. Amos could see the farmer's shadow growing longer just around the corner of the barn, stretching into the field as if claiming the land with its blackness. Then, he saw the familiar, faded back of Farmer Willis' overalls and the wide brim of his brown felt hat. In his right hand swung the oak-handled axe.

Amos stood frozen in the late afternoon shadows and watched as Farmer Willis turned the blunt end of the axe toward the dirt and scraped it along the hard ground in a long, slow streak. When he was done, he lifted the flat edge to his eye and examined it for a moment and then again dragged it hard across the dirt, cutting a shallow divot into the ground. When he was finished, he lifted his head and looked around, scanning the fields for the dog. Amos drew from his stupor and charged around the corner of the barn, dropping obediently to his haunches in front of the old farmer.

Farmer Willis stood there and looked down his nose at the old dog, the axe swinging gently at his side like a dying pendulum. His lips curled in a malignant sneer, and he stared at the old dog for a moment and then slowly turned his gaze toward the pasture. His eyes counted the cows — one, two, three, four, five, six, seven, eight, nine. When he was finished, he turned back toward Amos, and the scowl slowly melted into flat line and he spoke.

"Get on," was all he said, his tone gruff and low. The two brusque words liberated Amos, setting him free and rewarding him for a good day's work. He longed for nothing more than those two words. His mouth opened wide; he panted with excitement, a wordless thanks to the dispassionate old man. Then he turned and ran for the wood line to splash in the stream until the sun set and he would curl in his rotting dog house and sleep through the night.

"Thank you, Mister Amos," said Tibbitts as he finished his inquiries of the old dog, turned, and marched back toward his table.

Before Tibbitts had even finished flapping his wings to rise into his chair, Cyrus had edged to his seat and pounced to the floor. He slinked across the well of the courtroom like a predator, stalking toward Amos, who sat wide-eyed in the witness box, resting uncomfortably on his haunches on the hard, wooden chair. As Cyrus approached, the dog instinctively scooted backward, and a thin strand of drool dangled from the corner of his mouth. Aside from Amos' anxious panting, the courtroom was grave and silent.

In the jury box, the alabaster duck rose and then squatted, stretching his legs in preparation for a lengthy cross examination. The other jurors glanced about at the sudden movement, and many seized the opportunity to readjust themselves similarly. The big-bellied goat shifted awkwardly in his chair, and the turkey stretched his wings, lifting them gracefully for a moment and then tucking them neatly against his sides.

Before them, Cyrus paced slowly back and

forth across the wooden floor, allowing the anxiety to build in the old dog seated before him in the witness stand. After a moment, the audience stirred, restless for the show to begin. Cyrus paced several steps more, pushing the cold silence to its boundaries, and Amos began to squirm visibly in the chair. Small wisps of white hair shed from his flanks and floated gently to the courtroom floor. Amos looked toward Tibbitts with pleading eyes and then glanced toward Judge Fogel, as if desperate for someone to break the silence. Just as Judge Fogel leaned forward in his chair, Cyrus spoke.

"Mister Amos, good morning." His quiet, silky words melded seamlessly into the still silence of the courtroom, gracefully drawing the gallery's attention.

"G-g-good morning," Amos stuttered, glancing around nervously.

"I appreciate the *great detail* you have provided here today," said the cat, drawing out the words and lowering his eyes for a brief moment. "I'm sure you're aware of how details are important in a matter such as this." Cyrus lifted his gaze, and his eyes bored into Amos.

Amos nodded slowly, as if being commanded by the cat.

"You've been Samuel Willis' dog for many years?"

Amos nodded once more.

"Please say yes or no," admonished Judge Fogel gently, aware the dog was extremely nervous. Nonetheless, Amos' eyes drew wide, and he spun over his left shoulder at the voice.

"Yes, yes," said Amos quickly.

Cyrus took another step toward the witness box. "In fact, you've been on that farm your entire life, haven't you?"

Amos nodded again and then caught himself. "Yes, since I was born."

"And as you sit here today, you are how old, Mister Amos?"

Amos instinctively looked toward Willis, as if searching for an answer from his master, but Willis only stared back coldly. Amos was silent for a moment. "I believe I am twelve years old."

Cyrus paced toward the jury, nodding his head slowly at the answer. "Twelve years old," he said toward the jury. "Twelve years is a long life, isn't it, Mister Amos?"

Amos looked confused for a moment. "I suppose it is."

"Mister Amos, would you agree that, sometimes, when we get older, our senses start to fade?"

Amos scanned the room awkwardly. "I suppose so."

"In fact, your hearing isn't quite what it used to be, is it?" asked Cyrus, the words seeming to fade into the vacuum of the courtroom as he intentionally lowered his voice.

Amos leaned forward in his seat to hear the end of the question, as if on command. At the table, Willis' lips twitched upward in an almost imperceptible smile. The cat was wily.

"I can still hear just fine," said Amos, somewhat defensively.

Cyrus replied quickly, his tone sharpening suddenly. "Isn't it true that Samuel Willis would sometimes have to call for you several times to return from the creek?"

Amos stirred. "Whenever I heard him call, I came."

"Well then," Cyrus turned back toward Amos, "isn't it true that several times you returned from the creek and Samuel Willis *told you* that he had called for you many times?"

"Yes, sometimes he would say that," said Amos without hesitation.

"Then Mister Amos, does Samuel Willis have any reason to say falsely that he had called you numerous occasions?"

Amos thought for a moment. "I...I don't see why he would."

Cyrus seized on the reply. "Then will you concede that there have been times when Samuel Willis has had to call you more than once to return from the creek?"

Amos paused, his eyes focused in deep thought and then he nodded. "I suppose so."

"And that was because you did not hear him the first time?"

"I suppose so."

Cyrus moved slightly to his right, blocking Amos' view of Tibbitts. "Now, given your *hearing problems*," Cyrus paused for a long moment, letting the words sink into the courtroom, "isn't it quite possible that the noises you think you heard in the barn on the day in question were not really what you think you heard?"

Amos glanced down at the floor and then looked around, seemingly confused. "I don't know what you mean."

Cyrus answered sharply. "Mister Amos, isn't it entirely possible that these noises that you described as moans and a thud," he raised his paw as if signaling quotation marks, "were something entirely different? Perhaps something being moved or something dropped in the barn?"

Amos thought for a moment and then started to pant nervously. "I suppose it could have been, but I think I heard what I heard."

"You *think*!" Cyrus caterwauled suddenly.

"You *think* you heard Samuel Willis murdering the victim!"

Amos startled back in his chair at the sudden ruckus from the cat. The gallery buzzed with fervor, and dozens of angry eyes seemed to bore into the trembling dog.

"But are you *one hundred percent* certain in what you heard, Mister Amos?"

Amos looked perplexed. "No, I suppose not."

Cyrus continued, his tone becoming even more aggressive. "Now Mister Amos, you also claim that you saw Samuel Willis wiping blood from the axe?"

Amos struggled to regain his composure and barely nodded. Judge Fogel leaned forward, which was enough to stir him to answer. "Yes, sir," he said, still rattled.

"Mister Amos, at twelve years old, is it possible that, just like your *hearing,*" again, he drew out the words, "your eyesight is not what it once was?"

Amos squinted his eyes and blinked as if testing them for himself and then satisfied, said, "I can see good."

Cyrus stepped toward the jury box. "You can see *good*?" he repeated Amos' words, chiding the dog. "And again, are you are *one hundred percent* certain that you saw Samuel Willis wiping blood from the axe?"

Amos nodded.

Cyrus continued to press. "There is not one shadow of a doubt as to what you believe you saw that day?"

Amos nodded once more.

"Answer verbally, please," cautioned Judge Fogel.

"Yes, yes, I think so," said Amos sheepishly.

Tibbitts began to rise in his chair.

"You *think* so," Cyrus repeated the words again, this time softly.

Tibbitts tottered for a moment longer and then sat down.

"And Mister Amos, you said you were approximately forty feet from Samuel Willis when this incident happened. Is that right?" asked Cyrus.

"Yes, about that far."

Then Cyrus turned toward the gallery, his eyes scanning the crowd for a moment. The humans shifted uncomfortably in their seats at his gaze and turned, looking at each other to see what the cat was looking at.

"Mister Amos," he said after a moment, "in the back row of the gallery, in the third seat from the door is a man in a hat and a checkered shirt. Do you see him?"

Amos squinted his eyes and leaned forward in his chair. The audience glanced back and forth between Amos and the man in the back of the gallery, who looked suddenly ungrateful to be the focus of attention. Tibbitts turned in his chair and looked at the man in the gallery then back at Cyrus, his eyes narrowing to slits at the cunning cat.

Amos continued to stare into the gallery for a moment, peering forward to sift through the crowd. "I do see him," he said finally.

"Good," said Cyrus crisply, turning back toward Amos as the gallery's eyes followed him. "Now, I want you to tell me whether that man is wearing glasses or not."

The crowd turned once again to look at the man, whose face had grown a ruddy shade as he shifted in his seat. Instinctively, he touched the bridge of his nose and pushed a pair of thin, wire-framed glasses up the bridge of his nose.

Amos leaned forward once more, lowering his head and staring slack-jawed into the crowd. The humans buzzed with anticipation.

"Take your time," said Cyrus, his words dripping with insincerity.

Amos squinted again and blinked twice, focusing intensely. "He is not."

At the words, the crowd muttered among themselves, the humans gloating with righteous indignation and the animals stricken with consternation.

"There will be order in the courtroom," said Judge Fogel, his tone as loud as it had been the entire morning. After a moment, the muttering dropped to a murmur and then dissipated to silence.

Amos leaned back in his chair, glancing around the courtroom. His eyes landed on Tibbitts, who only shook his head slowly from side to side. The old dog seemed to wilt in his chair, and his eyes began to dart around anxiously, as if questioning everything about his account.

"Your honor, please let the record reflect that the witness was unable to see glasses on a man standing approximately forty feet from the witness stand," said Cyrus with the utmost formality, "the same distance Samuel Willis was when this witness allegedly saw the bloody axe." Once again, the crowd buzzed.

Judge Fogel lifted his head from Cyrus and spoke directly to the crowd, his tone loud and solemn. "The record will so reflect that the witness was unable to identify glasses on the man in the back of the gallery."

For a fleeting moment, the old bailiff dog's stoic demeanor vanished before his visible disappointment in his fellow canine. Amos lowered his head in embarrassment.

"So Mister Amos," said Cyrus, "it seems that your account of the day, may be somewhat...shall we say...*questionable*."

Cyrus paced back across the floor and stood in front of the table by Samuel Willis. "Now, I'd like to talk about a few other things," he said, sounding suddenly chipper. "Will that be alright?" he asked rhetorically.

Amos, still looking down, nodded his head up and down. Judge Fogel said nothing. The dog was defeated enough.

"I'd like to talk about your character, Mister Amos," said the cat, suddenly glowering at him.

Amos looked up suddenly.

"Mister Amos, in order for this jury to believe your story, they should be convinced that you are a trustworthy, decent, and honorable dog," he said, his delivery smooth and buttery. He paced back across the courtroom and stood at the far end of the jury.

"Mister Amos, on March 25th, did you or did you not kill a chicken belonging to the neighbor, Farmer Broadus?" he asked, the words sharp and direct.

The animals stirred in their seats. The duck, seated just feet from Amos, looked suddenly nervous. Beside him, the two dingy chickens ruffled their feathers and glanced anxiously about the room, their heads bobbing forward and back.

"I did," said Amos, embarrassed.

The chickens clucked and stared at the old dog, their beaks agape.

"Mister Amos," said Cyrus, the questions coming in staccato fashion, "on June 17th of last year, did you or did you not chase the school children on their way home from the bus stop?"

Amos hunched in his chair, his head bowed again as if contemplating. There was a long pause.

"Mister Amos, if you are having trouble recollecting, Miss Dowell, who lives near the bus stop, is in the audience today and would be happy to refresh your memory," he said, turning and looking into the gallery at a frumpy, older woman in a red floral dress, who appeared ever-so-eager to step to the witness stand and recount her story.

"I did," said Amos in a whimper.

Cyrus smirked to himself. Willis moved to the edge of his chair, engrossed in the theater.

"And Mister Amos, on August 5th of this year, did you or did you not cause injury to one sheep while herding it back to the pasture by biting the animal unnecessarily on the leg?"

Willis eyed the old dog, who looked like he might crumble at any moment. Amos' head started to rise and fall in a slow nod. "I did."

Cyrus stepped forward to the corner of the witness stand, only inches from Amos. "Mister Amos, you told this fine jury that you thought you heard a thud and moaning from the barn, but now you're not one hundred percent sure."

Amos nodded somberly.

"You claimed that you saw blood on Samuel Willis' axe, but you failed to see a man with glasses just feet from this witness stand."

Amos nodded again.

"And you somehow expect this jury to believe you today?"

Amos closed his eyes, longing for the moment to pass.

"You expect this jury to believe a killer of chickens, a chaser of children, and a biter of sheep!" he howled at the timid dog.

Tibbitts jumped to his feet. "Objection, your honor!"

"Nothing further for the witness, your honor," said Cyrus coolly as he cut his eyes toward Tibbitts and, with a devilish sneer, strutted gracefully back to the defense table, hopping silently back into his chair and curling to a comfortable rest beside Willis.

CHAPTER 5

I t took several tense minutes for the clamorous crowd to settle after Amos had left the courtroom. On his way out, the humans jeered and howled, raining ugly epithets upon him from both ends of the benches. Across the aisle, the animals looked forlorn and disenchanted with the old dog, and many moved away from the aisle or turned their eyes and noses away from him as he passed. Even the old bailiff dog did little to hide his chagrin as he led Amos down the aisle, his brow furrowed in overt disgust. Only a single, young pig seated at the edge of the bench near the door seemed to offer the old dog any sympathy, nosing his snout into Amos' fur as he passed in a simple gesture of support.

Finally, when the old bailiff dog returned to the courtroom and took his position just inside the double doors, Judge Fogel lifted his head to observe the crowd, peering out into the lower gallery and then up to the balcony where a disheveled row of the smaller animals — not the cows and equines whose weight might prove too much for the balcony — gawked down at the proceedings. Chickens nosed their beaks through the vertical, wooden rails, and lanky goats leered bug-eyed over the railing, occasionally gnawing at the lacquered wood before some other animal in the gallery would nudge them sharply with a wing or a hoof to discourage the behavior.

"Please be seated," said Judge Fogel in a deep, clear voice. At once, the humans and animals alike took their seats on haunches and buttocks or whatever manner was most comfortable. "Your next witness, Mister Tibbitts," added Fogel, nodding down at the rooster.

Tibbitts fluttered down from his chair, seemingly determined to undo the damage that his wily opponent had done on the prior witness. He turned toward the double doors and nodded at the bailiff. "Mister Horace," he said resolutely.

The old bailiff dog pushed through the double doors again and vanished for a moment. After a brief silence, the doors swung open again, and the old donkey hobbled through, his once-beige fur now mostly white, with two tired, coal-black eyes set below a pair of furry tuft brows. The donkey stared straight ahead as he plodded along, the clunking of his hooves on the noisy floor echoing off the walls of the small courtroom. The crowd —

humans and animals alike — seemed to pay a somber reverence to the old creature as he trudged along and pushed through the small double doors with his broad chest, then moved to the witness stand and stood waiting. The old bailiff dog circled around and pushed the chair aside with his shoulder and then stepped back. The donkey moved gingerly into the witness box.

"Mister Horace?" asked Judge Fogel.

The old donkey stopped before entering the witness box and turned tediously to look at Judge Fogel. "No, your honor — a donkey, not a horse."

Judge Fogel closed his eyes ever-so briefly as if to maintain his composure then simply nodded. "Yes, I see that. Your name is Mister *Horace*?" he asked, enunciating the word.

"It is," said the donkey. His voice creaked like a rusted hinge. Then he ambled into the witness box and rested backward, his rear legs splayed out beneath the table before him, and his front legs pressed straight and firm into the wooden platform.

"Mister Horace, do you swear to tell the truth, the whole truth, and nothing but the truth?" asked Judge Fogel.

"I do," said Horace somberly.

Tibbitts moved forward from where he stood at the defense table, approaching within just a few feet of the donkey.

"Good morning, Mister Horace," he said. "Or is it quite afternoon?" he asked, glancing at the clock that now read 11:24 AM. "Morning it is," he confirmed.

Horace allowed him to finish and then slowly nodded his long head. "Good morning."

"Mister Horace, I'd like to take you back to the day after the incident in question if I may — September 3rd," said Tibbitts gently, as if talking reverently to an elder. "Do you recall where you were that day?"

Horace nodded ponderously. "I was in the field preparing to plow."

"So you were one of Samuel Willis' animals?"

"I was."

"And how long had you been on that farm?"

Horace lifted his head and surveyed the crowd. "For most of fifty years." Judge Fogel leaned forward in his seat and studied the old donkey, seemingly impressed at his longevity.

Tibbitts backpedaled toward the jury box. "And you regularly plowed the field?"

"I did," said Horace. "My whole life." A hint of defeat crept into his voice.

"Will you tell us about that day in the field, Mister Horace?"

Horace studied Tibbitts as he spoke, as if the

events of that day had begun to carve a long, painful passage through his mind. He nodded his head and began to recount the day, the words slow and deliberate.

On the field atop the bluff overlooking the farm, Horace stood alone. His weary eyes gazed into the distance, beyond the red barn and the milking parlor, and settled upon the white, clapboard house that rose from a small stand of juniper trees. Above, the billowy clouds drifted lazily across the pale morning sky, pushing their way toward the amber sun that had just begun to peek over the horizon.

The old farm dog, Amos, circled nearby in the field, searching the tattered wire fence for gaps where the lingering sheep on the other side might escape. When the dog had finished, he sprinted back across the field, passing Horace with the casual glance of two creatures who had done this routine many times before. Then, he crouched and leapt over the fence and galloped down the hill toward the barn.

In the still morning, Horace heard the unceremonious screech of the metal screen door far in the distance. The old donkey gazed down the hill and, through his cataracts, could see the shape of Farmer Willis pulling on a thin jacket and then tightening the laces on his boots. The old man turned and marched toward the hill, his eyes falling on the old donkey who waited dutifully next to the plow that lay in the dirt where Farmer Willis had left it the day before.

Horace stamped his feet, assessing the firmness of the ground. The dirt was hard, and he knew the day ahead would be long and arduous. For nearly fifty years, he had worked this farm, plowing the fields, carrying loads of hay on his back, and fending off the coyotes and red foxes who roamed in from the nearby woods, searching for quarry. But today, he was tired. His back ached from laboring the day before, and his old joints were sore and swollen. He longed only to go lay in the pasture in the shade of the broad, leafy branches and rest; he had worked long enough. But there was no rest this day. Farmer Willis seemed to care nothing that the old donkey had turned white and moved slower than he ever had before. It seemed that the old man would drag every ounce of labor from the poor animal.

The stomping of Farmer Willis' boots roused Horace from his thoughts, and he shook his head vigorously to steel himself for the labor ahead. He resolved to push the aches and soreness from his mind and hoped only that, when night fell, he might lie his creaking body down on the small patch of grass and sleep to the sound of the old barn owl.

Farmer Willis pushed on the rotting, wooden gate, and the door swung open, lopsided on bent hinges. The whole farm was that way — crooked and crumbling — buildings, animals, and all. The last decade had been hard for all who resided here, and Horace knew it more than most. Unlike most of the others, who grew only old enough for slaughter or until they ran dry of milk, Horace had been here since time immemorial. Many years ago, the farm had prospered. The rich fields teemed with crops, the red barn stood crisp and fresh against the azure sky, and the white clapboard house seemed to shimmer against the pastures as if taken from the canvas of some rustic painting. And the animals, as miserable as they might have been with their lot in life, were fat and fed with beds of fresh straw and clear water in their pails and troughs.

Things had changed a decade ago. The great factories had sprung up around the nearby city, showering the people of Plum Grove and other neighboring towns with foods and wares and everything they could possibly dream of. Old farmers, like Samuel Willis, soon went by the wayside, fading into obscurity. All around this place, most of the neighbors had folded, closed their farms, sold their land, and took "real" jobs in the city.

Across the once quaint countryside, clapboard houses just like Farmer Willis' were torn down to make way for sprawling homes, and the city folk filled the countryside with their fancy cars and drab, pale children. But farming was in Samuel Willis' blood, and he knew no other way.

Horace remembered the times well when Farmer Willis would stumble into the fields late, well after the sun had nearly crested in the sky, stinking of the human's liquor. He would stagger and struggle to put the harness around the old donkey, and the two would totter along the field, barely digging an inch into the rocky soil. Sometimes Farmer Willis would wobble and fall down in the field, cursing and blustering about some phantom rock or divot. Dutifully, Horace would lower his long nose and nuzzle the man, offering some unspoken comfort as he lay there writhing in the dirt, fighting with the demons inside him.

The old donkey would never forget the day Farmer Willis' wife left the farm. As was his routine, Horace had stood there in the pasture, high on the bluff, waiting. He heard the old metal storm door rattle and then slam hard against the frame of the clapboard house.

"Don't you ever call me, you sonofabitch!" she had screamed, her voice sprawling across the pastures. The sheep startled at the racket and stopped their grazing to watch the spectacle unfold. With those words, she stormed across the well-trodden driveway, her blue floral dress drifting angrily in the wind, and opened the door of her little black car. Horace could hear the engine start in a hurry, then the door slammed, and a puff of dust blew from her wheels as she raced away and disappeared.

Things grew even worse after that day. Every day thereafter, the old man was even angrier, and the animals could never seem to work hard enough or produce enough to satisfy him.

Today would no doubt be another such day, thought Horace, as Farmer Willis stomped into the pasture. The breeze was free of alcohol, and only the dank scent of the man's odor carried across the distance to Horace's wide nostrils.

The morning sun lit a path before him, and he strode toward the old donkey. A broad, felt hat covered his head, set atop a pair of determined eyes, crisp blue with crow's feet stretching far along the weathered skin on either side. His chin was firm and set forward as if he were determined this day that the field would be plowed no matter what. Over a dirty blue, button-up shirt, the old man wore a pair of denim overalls. A thin, unlit cigarette dangled precariously from his thin, wicked lips.

"You ready to work today," he said, a statement not a question.

Horace hung his head, and in his mind, he could feel every ache of his tired joints. Farmer Willis lifted the straps from the plow and quickly cinched the harness around the old donkey. When he was finished, he raised his arm and slapped Horace hard on his flank. "Get on!" he yelled abrasively. And with that, Horace stepped one hoof before the other and slowly plodded across the hard dirt while Farmer Willis guided the plow from behind.

For four hours, they toiled without pause. The sun rose high in the sky, its rays soaking into the depths of Horace's coarse fur. The old donkey's mouth gaped open, gasping for air, yet he pushed onward, his long, knobby legs occasionally buckling on a rock or small rise in the ground. Eventually, he could go no further, and he stopped in the field. Behind him, he heard the plow totter and fall to the ground as Farmer Willis struggled to keep it upright. When the metal hit the ground with a thud, there was a cold silence, breached only occasionally by the drumming of an industrious woodpecker laboring on a distant cottonwood tree.

Then, Horace heard Farmer Willis' boots stomping once more as he marched up beside the old donkey on his left and stood there, staring at him slack-jawed, the unlit cigarette now-soggy and stuck to his bottom lip.

"You're asking for it today, aren't you?" he asked, his voice low but menacing. The old man swiveled his head from side to side as if sizing Horace up. Horace stood there stoically, staring straight ahead; he had been through this before. Every inch of his old body throbbed, and his mind sparked and sputtered, trying to will his body forward, but he simply could not.

Farmer Willis stood there beside him, his body tense and his hands at his side balled into fists. The veins on his forearms rippled beneath his ruddy, wind-weathered skin. "You gonna make me do to you what I did to that old heifer yesterday, aren't you?"

Then suddenly, Farmer Willis cocked his right arm and glared at Horace, who began to tremble and brace himself for the blow. For a long moment, the old man held his arm cocked and aimed at the side of Horace's long head. Horace closed his eyes and focused on the sound of the woodpecker, hoping the distant knocking on the old cottonwood could somehow carry him far from this place.

"You been with me a long time," snarled Willis. "Don't make me do you like that, you old mule," he growled. And then, Horace could hear his feet thudding back across the ground to the plow, and he heard the metal plow lift from the ground as the reins twisted and tightened on his back. "Get on!" yelled Willis, and somehow, Horace mustered the energy to move forward and finish the field, pushing his body beyond anything he had ever done before.

The sound of Tibbitts clawed toes clicking across the wooden floor brought Horace back from that day to the courtroom. The rooster strutted from the edge of the jury box back to the center of the floor and then the clicking stopped — he let the jury simmer in the old donkey's words for a moment.

"Thank you for your testimony today, Mister Horace," he said then turned to nod at the old donkey and stepped slowly back to his table.

Without hesitation, the old gray-white cat approached silently across the courtroom floor. "Hello, Mister Horace." The pleasantry was hollow.

Horace nodded long and slow. He had never trusted the cat.

Cyrus started in immediately. "You say that you were quite tired that day. Isn't that right?"

"Yes," purposely scarce with his words. He knew the old cat would try to lead him down a trail just as he had with the old farm dog, Amos, who had emerged from the courtroom looking frazzled.

"You said your body ached?"

"Yes."

"In fact, you said you were exhausted?"

"Yes."

"Worn out?"

Horace nodded.

"Mentally and physically?"

Horace nodded and said, "Yes," aware of Judge Fogel edging closer on the bench behind him.

"Your mind was . . . shall we say . . . not terribly alert?"

"Yes," acknowledged Horace, begrudgingly.

"And after a long day in the field, beneath the blistering sun, mentally and physically exhausted, you believe you heard Mister Willis say something?"

Horace opened his mouth, but before he could answer, Cyrus continued.

"Four long hours pulling a plow back and forth across the hard dirt, is that right?"

"That's right."

"And you told this jury that you were *mentally unfit* to work even before those four hours. Isn't that right, Mister Horace?" Cyrus pressed closer to the witness stand, his pitch rising with skepticism with each question.

Tibbitts rose quickly from his seat and squawked. "Objection, your honor! The witness did not say he was mentally unfit. Mister Sutton is mischaracterizing the prior testimony."

Judge Fogel turned and looked at Cyrus with an expression that showed he clearly agreed with Tibbitts.

"Your honor, pardon me," said Cyrus, then he turned back toward Horace. "After you already told this jury that you were both *physically and mentally exhausted* to begin with?" He turned and smirked at Tibbitts.

Tibbitts' feathers bristled, but he sat down begrudgingly in his chair.

"Yes," said Horace, reluctantly.

"But despite your mental and physical exhaustion," said Cyrus, his voice rising as he walked smoothly toward the jury, "and despite an additional four hours of hard work in the field, directly under the sun, and despite the fact that you have told this jury that you felt ill, you felt faint, your vision was beginning to blur, and your heart raced," he paced the length of the bannister before the jury, "despite all of those things, you are certain that you heard precisely what Mister Willis said to you that day?" he asked, his tone theatrically incredulous.

Horace allowed Cyrus to finish and then slowly lifted his head, his deep, black eyes connecting defiantly with the yellow slit eyes of the cagey feline. "That is correct, Mister Sutton," he said without hesitation. "I may just be an old donkey, sir, but I know what was said."

Cyrus averted his gaze, and he seemed to shrink a bit beneath the stare from the donkey. Feigning nonchalance, he sauntered back to his table, and with his back turned to Judge Fogel and the witness stand, he said simply, "Nothing further, your honor."

Tibbitts rose in his chair, his eyes fixed approvingly on Horace, and waited until Cyrus was seated. He allowed the faint buzzing of the crowd to subside and then cleared his throat. Judge Fogel looked down from the bench at the rooster, his eyes granting permission to speak.

"Your honor, at this time, the Animals rest," said Tibbitts resolutely.

Across the room, Willis shifted anxiously in his chair. The weight of the case now rested with Cyrus Sutton and the defense. Throughout the courtroom, the humans and animals brimmed with eager anticipation.

"Very well," said Judge Fogel, the crowd still murmuring anxiously as he spoke. He peered intensely over the heads of the gallery on to the old clock that ticked lifelessly high on the wall above the balcony. Narrowing his deep, onyx eyes to slits, he spoke once more. "Court is adjourned for exactly one hour. Do not be late," he added with finality and then hopped noisily down from the bench and disappeared through the rear door, his black robe trailing behind him.

After Judge Fogel had departed the courtroom, the old bailiff dog strode dutifully to the defense table and waited beside Willis. Cyrus whispered a few words of encouragement as the old man stooped over to listen, then nodded for him to follow the bailiff dog. Willis rose stiffly on tired legs and shuffled meekly toward the rear door as the old bailiff dog followed. Soon, the pair disappeared into the shadows and vanished from the courtroom.

CHAPTER 6

O utside, the hallway buzzed with excitement as the motley crowd filtered out discordantly, a disparate gaggle of fur, feather, and skin. People and animals jostled passively for position as they exited the benches and filtered into the hallway. The few women in the crowd turned their noses up in exaggerated gestures as the animals —most the barnyard variety — filtered in alongside them. The men scowled and muttered beneath their breath, and it was a wonder no scuffles erupted in the absence of the surly, old bailiff dog.

Tibbitts stood by the table, waiting patiently for the crowd to disperse. After the bailiff dog had secured Willis in the single, seldom-used holding cell of the Plum Grove Courthouse, he returned and escorted the jury through the door as the crowd filed out. The strange assembly of creatures shuffled through the doorway in a large, bustling herd, some looking over their shoulders at the dwindling crowd in the courtroom as if they expected a fight at any moment. Tibbitts stared down at his papers and shuffled them aimlessly with his beak, allowing the crowd to depart.

"You've got nothing, Tibbitts," hissed a familiar voice behind him. Tibbitts turned swiftly to the source of the sound and found Cyrus standing by the double doors to the gallery, looking quite hostile; his narrow yellowish eyes bored into him.

"Excuse me?" said Tibbitts, feigning as if he hadn't heard the cat's words.

"You won't get my man," said the cat, his words dripping with overt hostility. "Your witnesses didn't do you any favors — especially the dog," he spat.

Tibbitts turned away and looked back at his papers, shuffling them once more to enunciate his disinterest. Then, he lifted his head slightly and stared ahead to the rear door of the courtroom, not bothering to dignify the cat with his attention as he spoke. "We'll see what the jury has to say, Mister Sutton," he said, rather politely.

A faint, almost imperceptible growling noise brewed deep within the cat, just audible above the din of the last people and animals filing out of the courtroom. "I'll make you a deal, Tibbitts," snarled Cyrus.

Tibbitts turned slightly over his shoulder, looked at the cat impassively, and said nothing.

"Time served and we'll call it a day," said the cat bluntly.

Tibbitts lowered his head for a moment, and Cyrus continued. "Take it or we'll to bury you this afternoon, and these people will have you on a skillet before morning," he said, gesturing with his head toward the gallery.

Tibbitts raised his head slowly and let out a single, high-pitched cackle that startled the cat. "Mister Sutton," he chucked, "your *deal* is politely declined," he replied sardonically. "Your client will not escape justice as long as I am prosecuting this matter."

Cyrus sneered at the rooster. "You'll regret that when he walks, rooster," he grumbled dismissively and then pushed through the small double doors and into the hallway.

Outside in the hallway, the animals gathered at one end of the courthouse and the humans at the far end near the entrance. A small herd of Holsteins formed a protective half-circle around most of the other animals. At the center, the old donkey stood on wobbly legs, and the others seemed to pay him reverence for his steadfast performance on the witness stand. A rangy black and white goat showered him with praise. "Mister Horace," he bayed, drawing out the words, "I am most impressed with your performance today."

Nearby, a pair of turkeys warbled in agreement as the Holsteins nodded their heads up and down vigorously. In the far corner, Amos cowered and shivered as if he wished to hide from the other animals. Disloyal to his master and believing he let the other animals down, the old dog looked pitiful. But beside him stood the smallish pig, snorting and grumbling words of encouragement. His narrow, pinkish snout rubbed into Amos' side, reassuring him. Yet, the rest of the animals ignored him.

At the other end of the courthouse, the humans gathered and conversed heatedly in many small circles. Tall, wiry farmers, burly men from the stockyard, and a handful of women in their most fashionable dresses stirred, cursing Tibbitts and the animals in conspicuously loud tones.

The doors of the courtroom swung open, and Cyrus pushed his way out. As one, the animals turned and glowered at him. He looked away dismissively and pushed his way through toward the humans. As he approached, they opened their circles and allowed him to pass, some leaning low and patting him on his back. His tail arced high in the air as he strutted elegantly through the crowd and out the front door for some fresh air before court resumed.

After quite some time, the bailiff dog appeared in

the doors and bellowed, "Court will resume shortly!" The crowds began to mutter excitedly, and humans and animals alike made their way through the doors once more, passively pushing and jostling for position.

Tibbitts had never left the courtroom, content to sit at the table and pour over his notes. As the crowd settled in, the double doors swung open, and Cyrus returned. The crowd went quiet as he passed down the aisle and leapt gracefully into his seat next to Willis. Cyrus gave a quick, sharp glance toward Tibbitts, which the rooster promptly ignored.

Then, the old bailiff dog emerged from the rear door and called, "All rise!" Obediently, the crowd rose to their feet, hooves, and claws. The rear door swung open once more, and Judge Fogel entered, walking slowly to the chair, placing his front hooves up and then hopping his rear end into the seat. He settled in and scanned the crowd then nodded approvingly to the bailiff dog, who disappeared down the hallway once more. After a moment, the dog returned and held the door open as the jury filed into their seats, most looking deeply burdened at the grave responsibility bestowed upon them.

Once they had settled into their seats, Judge Fogel spoke. "Mister Sutton, is the defense ready to present its case?"

"We are, your honor," said Cyrus confidently.

"Very well," said Judge Fogel, "you may call your first witness."

Cyrus glanced toward the old bailiff dog, who had already started dutifully across the courtroom to the back doors for the next witness.

"Your honor, the defense would like to call Melvin Bickers."

The bailiff dog disappeared once more into the hallway, and the crowd shifted in their seats, seeking comfort on the unforgiving wooden benches. Tibbitts rested comfortably in his chair, no longer sifting through papers, but staring ahead past Judge Fogel. He did not look up when the doors opened and the old bailiff dog nodded his head for the witness to enter.

With purpose, a tall, barrel-chested man walked down the aisle toward the well of the courtroom. Clad in tattered, dark blue overalls and a thick white cotton shirt, he exuded the presence of a man who knew nothing but hard work his whole life. His chin was coated with a thick, coarse beard, sans mustache, that gave him the impression of some crusty old ship's captain. As he neared the double doors, he reached up and removed his broad felt cap and nodded his thick, balding skull at Judge Fogel in a sign of respect.

His weathered boots pounded firmly on the wooden floor, and he seemed eager to take the stand.

In the crowd, a few humans whispered unintelligibly, but most remained silent. The hulking man stepped up on the witness stand, towering above Judge Fogel, seated just over his shoulder. The chair squeaked harshly as he dragged it across the floor to make room and then plopped down roughly as if settling in for pints of ale at the Plum Grove Tavern.

When he was settled, Judge Fogel administered the oath and nodded toward the defense table.

Cyrus leapt down from his chair and sauntered across the floor. The man craned his head over the table at the approaching cat and set his thick, firm jaw in preparation for the questioning.

"Good afternoon, Mister Bickers."

"'Afternoon, Mister Sutton," said the man, with a seemingly practiced familiarity.

"Will you please state your name and occupation for the jury?"

The man twisted in his seat to look at the jury. His mouth opened briefly and then closed as if the surprise of addressing this bizarre collection of farm animals almost startled him, although he gave only the slightest outward appearance. Then he spoke. "My name is Melvin Bickers. I've been driving the slaughter truck for thirty years."

In the gallery behind the prosecution table, the animals stirred suddenly as if the words had caused a palpable fear. A chicken flapped his wings subconsciously, and a goat bleated fearfully. Bickers couldn't help but notice the commotion and turned to look to the crowd. As he did, his eyes narrowed like a discerning hawk peering down at a field mouse below.

"So, you're...uh...familiar with animals?" said Cyrus, awkwardly attempting to redirect him.

"Yes, sir. I've been driving that truck since I was sixteen years old. Took over when my old man passed away."

"And you've certainly dealt with your share of cows?"

"I have."

"You've probably seen cows in all sorts of conditions, haven't you?"

"I have," said Bickers simply.

"Healthy cows?"

"Yes."

"Sick cows?"

"Yes."

"Injured cows?"

"Yes," said Bickers, the two going back and

forth in a rhythmic cadence.

"Cows that have been stepped on?"

"More than a few," said Bickers, lifting his gaze to look into the jury, as if emphasizing the statement.

Cyrus nodded and paused for a moment before continuing. "Now, did you have occasion to visit Samuel Willis' farm on September 3rd?"

Bickers turned back toward the cat and nodded affirmatively. "Yes, I did."

"And you were there on business?"

"Yes, sir."

Cyrus turned and looked toward Willis, who sat engrossed in the testimony. "How long have you known Samuel Willis?"

Bickers lifted his hand to his chin and looked to the ceiling as if searching back in his memory. "I must've known Sam for close to the whole time I been driving that truck," he said and looked out toward Willis with a reassuring gaze.

"What kind of man would you say Samuel Willis is?"

Tibbitts stirred in his seat.

"Sam Willis is a damn good man," said Bickers, his words almost angry as he turned and looked toward the animals in the gallery. "It's a fine shame he's been brought in here like some common criminal," he huffed.

Cyrus stepped quickly toward the witness stand and placed himself in Bicker's view and gently redirected Bickers. "Have you ever known Samuel Willis to mistreat his animals?"

"Never," said Bickers firmly. "Never," he said again, shaking his head emphatically from side to side. His lips pressed firmly together, and the jawline beneath his beard pulsed.

"Have you ever picked up an animal from Samuel Willis that you thought had been abused?"

"No, sir," said Bickers. "Every animal I've gotten from that farm in thirty years been cared for just as they should."

Again, the animals in the gallery stirred at his words. At the end of the jury box, the tawny goat shifted uncomfortably. Cyrus glanced quickly at the jurors and then moved along with the questions.

"Back to September 3rd," he said, "when you arrived at Samuel Willis' farm, what was your purpose?"

"I was there to pick up a cow."

"When you say pick up a cow, do you mean a living cow?"

"No, sir," replied Bickers. "Sam called me the night before. Said he had a cow that had died, and he wanted to get it to the slaughterhouse 'fore it spoiled."

Cyrus paused for a moment, processing the answer carefully. "Do you recall about what time he called you?"

Bickers thought for a moment, his large hand again coming to rest on his beard. "Probably around 7:00 PM. The house phone rang, and the old lady said Sam was on the phone."

"I see," said Cyrus thoughtfully. "And did he tell you what had happened to this cow?" he asked, looking up at Bickers with a lowered head as if to emphasize the importance of the question.

Bickers started to nod slowly and then gazed firmly toward the humans in the crowd. "He said it had been stepped on," he said confidently. In the gallery, several people nodded in approval as they looked back at him.

Tibbitts sat in his chair motionless, seemingly unmoved by the examination.

"Stepped on, you say?" said Cyrus, emphasizing the answer.

"That's right," affirmed Bickers. "He said it got stepped on by another cow leaving the milking parlor. Crushed her skull right through."

In the gallery, several of the Holsteins twisted in their seats, looking incredulous at each other.

Cyrus nodded thoughtfully and paused for several seconds to allow the jury to process.

"Now, what time did you arrive at the farm the next day?"

"I woke up early to get there by 6:00 AM," he said. "Didn't want to let it sit out too long, else the meat wouldn't be any good."

Cyrus' whiskers crinkled at the answers, and he hurried on to his next question.

"And when you got there, what exactly did you see?"

Bickers shifted in his chair as if getting comfortable for a prolonged explanation. "Well, Sam greeted me out by the barn as I pulled up. He takes me into the barn, and I see *it* there," he said, the word carrying across the courtroom with a certain harshness. "Splayed out, legs goin' every direction. I walk up to it, and I could see it, giant hole in her skull where a cow's hoof done come down on her. Crushed right through her head, no question about it," he added.

Cyrus walked slowly toward the jury box. "Did you have a chance to examine this cow?" he said, choosing his words carefully.

"I did," replied Bickers. "Looked it all over before I loaded it up on the truck. You know, make sure everything else was in good shape."

"And you're certain the blow to the head was from a hoof?"

"I'm certain of it." He looked out to the crowd

again and lifted his hand to his face. "You could see the marks down its nose where that cow that killed it dragged its hoof over its head."

"Did Samuel Willis say anything to you that day about what had happened?"

Bickers nodded and his eyes tightened. "He told me that the last cow outta the parlor stepped on its skull," he said, his eyes connecting with Willis.

"And did you remove the deceased cow from the farm that day?"

Bickers nodded. "Sam and I used the winch to drag it up into the truck, and I took it straight to the slaughter plant," he said then opened his mouth as if to finish his thought.

Cyrus interjected before he could. "Thank you, Mister Bickers," he said hurriedly before the man could elaborate any further. "Thank you," he said again.

Then Cyrus lifted his head and looked at Judge Fogel. "Your honor, I have no further questions for Mister Bickers."

Bickers glanced over his shoulder at Judge Fogel as if discerning the next step in the proceeding while Cyrus turned and walked back to his table.

"Mister Tibbitts, your witness," said Judge Fogel.

Tibbitts shuffled his papers with his beak for

a moment and then hopped down from the chair, striding quickly to the center of the courtroom. Bickers stared down his nose with unmasked disdain at the rooster, the indignation of being cross examined by a fowl apparent on his face.

"Good afternoon, Mister Bickers," opened Tibbitts.

Bickers simply stared at the rooster and said nothing. Tibbitts stepped a pace closer to the man, who seemed to bristle in the witness chair at the bird's approach.

Tibbitts looked up and stared Bickers in the eye accusingly. "Mister Bickers, did actually *see* what happened to the victim?"

"I didn't need to see what happened. Was plain as day," he retorted.

"So the answer is no, you did not see what happened, correct?" responded Tibbitts calmly.

"I said I didn't need to," he replied angrily.

Judge Fogel leaned forward in his chair. "Mister Bickers, please answer the question asked."

Bickers turned toward Judge Fogel, seeming surprised, then shifted back and looked at Tibbitts. "No, I didn't see it happen. But I know what happened."

"And you examined the injury?" asked Tibbitts.

"Yeah, I looked at it real close. You could almost

see the hoof print in the skull," he said, again tracing his forehead with his finger.

"Mister Bickers, you have no veterinary training, do you?"

"I don't need no training to know when a damn cow's hoof smashes a skull," he replied sharply.

"So your answer is 'no.' Is that correct, Mister Bickers?"

"I don't have any vet training, roost—" he spat then cut himself off.

Tibbitts glanced toward the jury, gauging their reaction and then continued, "Mister Bickers, you said you've been dealing with the defendant for thirty years?"

"That's right."

"You know him well," said Tibbitts, a statement more than a question.

"Yeah."

"He's been a customer for a long time?"

"Yeah," said Bickers, growing impatient.

"He's always paid his bills?"

"Sam always pays his bills."

"Thirty years of bills?"

"Yeah," he said with more than a hint of frustration.

"Always paid them? For thirty years?"

"That's what I said," growled Bickers impatiently.

"If Mister Willis is found guilty here today, you are aware he may be hung?" The word lingered heavily in the courtroom.

"He ain't gonna be hung. Sam's an innocent man," retorted Bickers sharply.

"I'm sorry if my question was unclear, Mister Bickers," said Tibbitts patronizingly. "My question was whether you understood that, *if* he is found guilty, he may be hung?"

"I know what the punishment is," Bickers grumbled.

"And if Mister Willis is hung, you'd lose a customer of thirty years. Isn't that right?"

Bickers paused, and his lips twisted. "This ain't about losin' a customer," he snapped. "This is about that stupid cow stepping on a skull and you *animals* trying to make something bigger of it!"

Tibbitts allowed a calculated pause at the word before continuing. "Mister Bickers, you enjoy your work driving the slaughter truck, don't you?"

Cyrus shot up in his chair. "Relevance?!"

Before Judge Fogel could inquire, Tibbitts responded. "Your honor, the question goes to Mister Bickers' bias both in favor of Mister Willis and against the victim."

Judge Fogel contemplated for only a moment.

"I'll allow it. Repeat the question." He glanced at Cyrus, his eyes commanding the cat to sit.

Cyrus fumed silently and dropped heavily to his seat.

"You enjoy your work driving the slaughter truck, don't you, sir?"

Bickers brow furrowed in a look of consternation. For several seconds, he was silent, considering his response. "People gotta eat," was all he said.

Tibbitts lowered his eyes and glanced sideways at the jury. Satisfied, he swiveled back toward the witness stand, gave a polite, deferential bow to Bickers, and said simply, "Nothing further, your honor."

CHAPTER 7

C yrus collected himself then stood tall in his seat, clearing his throat; the white blaze of fur across his chest puffed outward with the bombastic gesture. "The defense calls Samuel Willis to the stand," he said grandly, making a production of the moment.

Once more, the crowd began to murmur, and Samuel Willis rose haltingly from his seat, adjusting the straps of his overalls as he stood on wobbly legs. He gazed down at the wooden floor for a moment as if collecting his thoughts, pushed his felt hat forward on the table, and began to tread slowly to the witness stand.

"Tell 'em the truth, Sam!" shouted a gravel-voiced farmer from deep in the gallery.

Others offered similar but indecipherable implorations. On the other side of the aisle, the animals stirred restlessly, the words of the humans seeming to rile and unsettle them.

Judge Fogel pounded his hoof rapidly on his bench with thinly veiled fury. "There will be order in the courtroom!" he demanded, his tone leaving no doubt of his sincerity. Quickly, the chorus of shouts and mutters faded to faint murmurs and soon to silence beneath Judge Fogel's beady, glowering eyes.

Samuel Willis turned toward Judge Fogel, who held his gaze on the gallery for a moment longer then turned toward the man, quickly administering the oath and gesturing for him to be seated.

Cyrus hopped down silently from his chair and casually paced several feet into the well of the courtroom. Several jurors moved to the edge of their seats — the anticipation of the defendant's testimony was palpable.

"Good afternoon, Mister Willis," began Cyrus cordially.

"Good afternoon," said Willis, an unsophisticated twang to his words.

"I'd like to start by having you tell the jury a bit about your background, your business, your family — those sorts of things," said Cyrus, his tone warm and buttery.

Willis nodded agreeably, his lips pressed firm in a straight, serious line like a man who knew how much was at stake. To his right, the afternoon sun strained through the dusty glass of the tall windows, and he squinted slightly as he looked out at Cyrus, occasionally glancing over the cat's his shoulder at his supporters, who sat on the edge of their seats in the far gallery.

"You've been a farmer most of your life, haven't you?" asked Cyrus.

"Yes, sir," said Willis, his demeanor plain and simple. "That farm been in my family close to sixty years. When my old man passed away, it come to be my 'sponsibility."

"*Responsibility*," said Cyrus, lingering on the word. "That's an interesting word. Tell us what that responsibility entailed?"

Tibbitts shook his head dismissively at the staged theater.

"Someone had to care for the land, the animals," he said, looking earnest. "This town wouldn't go on without farms like mine."

The farmers in the gallery nodded their heads vigorously and lowered their brows, urging Samuel Willis to share his truth.

"These people need to be fed. The land," he glanced out the tall window to the distant maize and sage-colored fields, "needs to be tended." He paused for a moment, gazing longingly far beyond the glass, and then continued. "Them animals need to be cared for to provide for this town."

Cyrus rested comfortably on his haunches

about ten paces from Willis, near the center of the jury box. "It's safe to say that your farm is a source of pride, is it not, Mister Willis?" he asked, serving up the question.

"That farm is all I have, sir," responded Willis, his eyes shifting downward toward the floor in a burgeoning expression of grief. "Since Delores left me, that farm was all I had." He wiped at his eye with his sleeve. "Them animals, too."

In the gallery, a turkey warbled dismissively. Judge Fogel raised his head and glared across the courtroom. Cyrus paused until silence settled over the room once more.

Willis wiped again at the corner of his eye, this time with the heel of his hand. "Take your time," said Cyrus, unnecessarily. Willis pressed his thumb and forefinger against the corner of each eye and sniffled softly.

"Mister Willis, now that we understand how much the farm and the animals mean to you," he added, as if asserting a universal truth, "I'd like to talk about the day in question."

Willis looked down at the wooden floor in front of him and nodded somberly. Over his shoulder, Judge Fogel peered down at him intently.

"Will you describe for the jury what happened that day?" said Cyrus.

Willis stared downward a moment longer. Then he lifted his head and looked across the courtroom, his gaze passing over the people and the animals and resting on a blank spot on the wall, and he began to recant his story.

Like every other milking day, the cows shuffled into the parlor and took their spots in the milking chutes. The old dog, Amos, had helped shepherd them in, but today, they seemed to be in good spirits and took very little coaxing. One by one, Samuel Willis secured their tethers to the iron fence that separated them.

Times had been hard since Delores had left him, but grit and determination afforded him a scant living off the old farm. Dairy was in his family, and he knew no other way. In fact, these cows were his family — every one of them — and without them, there would be no dairy. And with no dairy, there would be no farm.

That day, Samuel Willis stood in the milking parlor admiring the Holsteins. They certainly weren't the prettiest of the lot. Most of the girls were older and had worked on the farm for many years, but that only helped Samuel Willis bond with them. He knew them each by name and felt a special kinship with every one. As he attached their straps to the metal rails, he rubbed his hand down their backs and told them today would be a good day. He appreciated them for what they gave him, and he let them know that day.

As he worked his way down the aisle, he reached the old cow, Ofelia, and started to attach the milking equipment. He noticed that she had walked a little slower than the others, and Amos had to nip at her once to move her along, but it wasn't unusual for a cow to amble a little slower than the others on any given day.

But stepping into the aisle to attach the milking equipment, he saw her leg wobble. Concerned, he moved close to her and rubbed his hand down her side, reassuring her as he always did. She wobbled once more.

"You ok, old girl?" he said to her gently. Her eyes swiveled and looked at him, and he could tell at that moment she wasn't well.

"We're going to let you rest today," he said, rubbing his hand down her side again. He unfastened her tether and coaxed her slowly out of the aisle. As he did, she stumbled slightly but regained her footing. The other cows turned their heads and looked, growing concerned.

"It's ok, girls," he said, reassuring them as he gently guided Ofelia back down the aisle. "She's just going to go wait for us in the stall outside."

The two of them, like a father guiding his sick child, walked slowly down the aisle out the door.

Ofelia wobbled once more, and he knew something was wrong. Just as he made it through the door into the barn, she tottered, and he could see her legs begin to buckle.

"It's ok, girl," he said more urgently, rubbing his hand along the side of her face. "It's ok. Just you go ahead and lay down right here." He took the harness and slowly guided her to the first stall and bent his knees with her as her legs folded, and she slowly collapsed on the ground in a pile of hay with an exhausted huff. The old cow rested halfway in the stall and halfway in the aisle, but Farmer Willis let her rest there; he knew she needed it.

He crouched down beside her and rubbed his hands along her head, whispering softly to her. He could see a sickness in her eyes, although he wasn't quite sure what it was. Sometimes cows got sick — milk fever, probably. He sat crouched with her for a moment longer and then went and fetched a pail of water from the corner of the barn and rested it beside her, making sure she knew it was there.

"It's ok, girl," he said to her compassionately. "You take as long as you need." Then, he bent on creaky knees and stood there looking down at her.

After a moment, he returned to the milking parlor and milked the remaining nine cows.

Occasionally, he would check on Ofelia, glancing through the door or, on a few occasions, even walking out into the barn to make sure she was awake and alert.

When the other cows had been milked, he put the equipment away and walked out into the barn. He kicked the dirt and straw from the aisle, clearing a berth around Ofelia, who lay there, resting comfortably. He looked things over for a minute, making sure there was enough room to get the other cows around her. He was sure there was.

Then, one by one, he carefully led the cows out of the milking parlor, navigating them skillfully around Ofelia. Some of them stopped and sniffed, and he paused for a moment, and he let them share their moment. He led the first eight cows around her, and as each passed, he guided them into the small pasture just outside the barn door. After a moment, Amos appeared from the creek, and he smiled at the loyal dog and shook his head. *That old dog sure enjoys that creek.*

He returned to the milking parlor and unfastened the final cow, Geraldine. "Come on girl," he said to her. "You're going to have to watch your step coming out of the parlor." Then, he gently guided Geraldine from her stall and through the door, carefully navigating her around Ofelia.

Suddenly, the reigns tightened in his hand

and almost yanked him backward as Geraldine stumbled hard to her left, her front legs buckling and her head dipping violently toward the ground. She pressed her legs out to brace herself, and her front leg thrust downward in a panic, searching for the ground but instead finding the exposed crown of Ofelia's head.

Samuel Willis heard the sickening thud as the massive hoof shot outward like a piston. He could hear the bones of Ofelia's skull cracking as the breath blew out of her body in a painful moan. The pale whites of Geraldine's eyes shone in the shadowy barn as she stumbled, terrified, and finally found her footing, bracing her front feet on the ground.

It all happened so suddenly. Samuel Willis stumbled in the commotion but regained his footing and hurried Geraldine past him toward the barn door.

He rushed back to Ofelia and could immediately see the ribbons of bright red blood oozing from her skull onto the white patch of fur between her eyes. He dropped to his knees beside her and cradled her head. Her eyes rolled back and forth grotesquely; she was losing consciousness.

"No!" he cried as she breathed ragged breaths. He pressed his cheek against her, as if his warmth may will her to live, but he knew the wound was too grave. For a brief moment, she breathed deeply in short, warm breaths, blowing the hairs on his arm. Then, she wheezed mightily, and her lungs fell still. Her head went heavy and limp in his arms. For a long while, Samuel Willis sat there and held her as the tears rolled down his cheeks and soaked into her fur.

"Take your time, Mister Willis," said Cyrus as Willis sobbed openly on the stand. "I know this is difficult to relive."

The animals in the gallery muttered, and several flapped their wings in visible displays of disgust. Across the aisle, several of the women dabbed at their tears with silk handkerchiefs.

After a pause, Cyrus continued. "Mister Willis," he said gently, "I want to be very clear for the jury." He paused for a moment before continuing. "Never once did you strike Ofelia. Is that correct?"

Willis lifted his head. His eyes were stained red, and his cheeks glistened in the afternoon light from the streaks of his tears. He looked up and down the jury box slowly, gazing each animal in the eye. "I never hurt Ofelia," he said sincerely through muffled sobs. "What I have told you today is God's truth." Then he lowered his head and began to weep, his chest rising and falling.

Cyrus allowed the moans to drift through the courtroom for a moment. Then he dipped his head reverently and spoke like a minister presiding over some melancholy affair. "Your honor, I have no further questions for Mister Willis."

Judge Fogel sat forward in his chair. Even the old sheep seemed mildly captivated with Willis' story, as it took him a moment to gather his thoughts. He lifted his head and looked at Tibbitts.

"Mister Tibbitts, your witness."

Tibbitts hopped from his chair softly, as if he dared not betray the presumed reverence of the moment. He stepped on outstretched claws deep into the well of the courtroom and stood there silently, wings crossed, waiting for Willis to compose himself. After several more seconds, Willis lifted his gaze from the floor, tilted his head, and wiped his tears on the shoulder of his shirt. Then he looked straight ahead, a shell of a man behind two mournful eyes.

"Good afternoon, Mister Willis," said Tibbitts, politely.

"Afternoon, Mister Tibbitts," said Willis, respectfully.

"Mister Willis, you said you've farmed that land for decades. Is that true?"

"It is, sir."

"And you've had lots of animals over those years, correct?"

"Yes, sir. I've had quite a few."

"Having had so many animals for so many years, you're probably quite aware of their behaviors, aren't you?" asked Tibbitts somewhat sharply.

"I'd say I am pretty good at understandin' the animals, sir."

"And you've had cows?" asked Tibbitts.

"Yes."

"Sheep?"

"Yes."

"Donkeys?"

"Yes, sir."

"Chickens?"

"Yes, sir."

"Pigs?"

"Yes, I've had pigs," said Willis with a faint hint of inquisitiveness at the questioning.

Tibbitts moved closer. "So it is safe to say that you've been around all of these animals?"

"Yes," answered Willis, his voice taking on a sharper edge.

"And you know when they're ill?"

"Most of the times," said Willis, slowly.

"But despite your decades of being around animals on that farm, somehow you did not know the victim, Ofelia, was sick before you paraded her into the milking parlor?" snapped Tibbitts.

Willis paused for a moment, thinking about

his answer. He lowered his head then spoke. "I didn't notice anything wrong with her 'til she was in the parlor," he answered. "Sometimes it happens that way."

"You didn't see her limping in the barn?"

"It's dark in that barn. If she was limpin', I didn't see it."

"You didn't see her limping on her way in from the pasture?" asked Tibbitts as he moved even closer, just feet from Willis now.

"Amos had them to the barn door by the time I got there," retorted Willis.

Tibbitts lifted his head and looked sharply at Willis, his black pupils rolling forward on his bulbous eyeballs. "You didn't herd the cows to the barn, Mister Willis?"

"I'd been up at the coop killin' chickens for market and come down just as Amos had them headin' into the barn," he answered.

The two chicken jurors shifted uncomfortably in their seats, and Willis' eyes darted to them. His expression shifted to one of regret for letting the words slip so casually.

Tibbitts allowed them to linger for a moment. "But you noticed something wrong with her in the milking parlor as you attempted to milk her?"

Samuel Willis nodded. "Like I said, I could see she wasn't feeling well when I went to fix on the equipment." His voice softened. "I tried to help her there in the parlor."

Tibbitts paced softly toward the jury box. "You tried to help her, you say? But isn't it true that, when you did finally notice something was wrong with her, you balled your fist and punched her in her side?" he asked, the words sharpening suddenly.

The courtroom stirred.

"I most certainly did not," barked Samuel Willis, his lips curling upward as he looked down at Tibbitts with intense indignation.

"You comforted her by punching her in the side. Is that how you did it, Mister Willis?" fired Tibbitts.

"No, sir! I did not!"

Tibbitts pressed onward. "She tottered in that stall, sick with — as you call it, *milk fever* — and almost fell over on you, didn't she?" He emphasized the words with a hint of disgust.

"No, sir. That did not happen," answered Willis, his tone calming slightly but the words still laced with disdain.

"And that made you angry," said Tibbitts, ignoring Willis' response. "And you curled your arm back," he said as he cocked his wing, "and you slammed your fist into her side." His voice rose dramatically as his wing flapped forward, mimicking the blow.

The audience buzzed behind Tibbitts, and Judge Fogel looked up over his snout at the gallery growing more raucous.

"I did no such thing, Mister Tibbitts!" said Willis defiantly. "I have *never* hurt my animals!" he bellowed, his voice seeming to rattle the panes of the tall window.

"That cow—" he started, spitting the words. "Geraldine…that's the one that should be on trial here today!" he bellowed, the veins bulging in his neck. "That's the one that stomped her damn hoof into Ofelia's skull and caused me all this trouble!" With the words, he slammed his fist into the witness stand, and the courtroom grew still.

Tibbitts let the words hang in the air, not daring to spoil the moment. Finally, the wind withdrew from Willis' puffed chest, and he slouched back in his chair, although his lips remained curled downward in a spiteful frown.

Tibbitts paused for just a moment longer and then continued. "Mister Willis, did you ever threaten your donkey, Mister Horace?"

Willis laughed mockingly. "That donkey's been with me as long as I can remember. Don't know what I'd do without him," he added fondly.

"Never told him he'd end up like the victim?"

"Never," said Willis firmly.

"So, Mister Horace is lying?"

"Yep," he said smugly.

"Just like Geraldine is lying?"

"Yep."

"Mister Willis," he started slowly, "let's talk about your farm dog, Mister Amos. He testified earlier."

"That dog's a damn liar," snarled Willis.

"I suspected you'd say that," said Tibbitts derisively with a slight flourish of his wing. "He testified that he heard Ofelia moaning in the barn after you entered."

"She was moaning 'cuz she got her skull crushed by that damn cow," he answered indignantly.

Tibbitts' tone softened. "And when Mister Amos testified that he saw you exit the barn with a bloody axe, that wasn't true?"

Willis seemed to roil at the question. "There wasn't no blood on it like that damn dog says. I hadn't even been up to the coop to kill them chickens yet," he huffed in exasperation.

Tibbitts looked up briefly, almost startled. His eyes gazed at Willis for a moment.

"That dog blind as a country bat," scoffed Samuel Willis with a slight chuckle.

"Mister Willis, moments ago, you told this jury," he said as he gestured in a sweeping motion with his wing, "that you arrived late to the barn because you had just finished slaughtering chickens for market." Tibbitts' voice rose to a crescendo. "*Now*, you've just told us that you did leave the barn with the axe after Ofelia moaned."

Willis' stared at Tibbitts for a moment, then his eyes darted left and right, his brain processing. He glanced downward.

"Which one is it, sir?" grilled Tibbitts, his voice as harsh and shrill as it had been all day.

Willis looked up over Tibbitts' shoulder into the gallery. "Musta been afterward," he said timidly. "Things start runnin' together when I get real stressed like this."

Tibbitts paced across the courtroom and then back to the jury box, his claws clicking in slow, staccato fashion on the hardwood floor, as if giving Willis time to stew on his words. Willis sat there silently in the jury box, realizing he had said enough.

After a long moment, Tibbitts looked up from the floor and scanned the jury with his eyes. The animals peered at the defendant, studying his face. Then Tibbitts turned, and his eyes connected with Willis before the old farmer broke his gaze and looked away.

"I have no further questions for Mister Willis, your honor," he said, after much contemplation.

Then he turned slowly and returned to his table.

Willis sat rigidly in the witness chair, his narrowed eyes following Tibbitts back to his seat.

Judge Fogel leaned forward over the bench. "Mister Willis, you may step down."

Willis startled at Judge Fogel's voice behind him. Then he rose from the witness box on shaky legs as if the experience had aged him a decade. He braced both hands on the table and stooped over for a moment, gathering himself. Then carefully, he stepped down with his right foot, his old leather boot resonating on the wooden floor in the silence of the courtroom. He brought his left foot down and stood upright, like a dilapidated old barn being raised from a dried-up pasture. He turned and gazed out into the courtroom, his eyes scanning the benches, seeking the strength of friendly faces.

"That's right, Sam!" muttered a disheveled young farmer from several rows deep.

"Yes, sir," said another with a resolve strengthened by the first voice.

Judge Fogel looked into the audience and studied the crowd but said nothing.

As Willis slowly tottered across the floor, the people buzzed in their seats. For the most part, the animals sat silently on the other side, although several snouts crinkled in sneers, and more than a few beady eyes cut glances at the farmer as he walked tediously to the defense table. Cyrus sat stoically in his chair, staring down as if focused on the next witness.

Outside the courtroom, the long, billowy clouds rolled across the pale blue sky, for a moment, blotting the sun and casting the courtroom in a long, dull shadow. In the balcony above, clawed feet and hooves shuffled as the animals shifted and moved to find more comfortable positions that seemed to elude them on the unforgiving benches.

From the front row, a speckled goat leaned forward over the railing and whispered. "Mister Tibbitts," he said in something of a croaking hiss. Tibbitts half-turned in his seat at the voice, and his eye raised dismissively at the interruption. But the goat leaned forward, craning his long neck over the railing, feverishly raising and lowering his head as if to beckon Tibbitts closer. Curious now, Tibbitts leaned over the rail of his chair, and the goat whispered in his ear.

Across the aisle, Samuel Willis slumped down in his chair, the weight of the moment causing his shoulders to sag down toward the wooden floor. Cyrus glanced at him only momentarily, cutting his eyes at the old man.

From the bench, Judge Fogel turned his gaze

toward Tibbitts and the goat and then cleared his throat conspicuously and then spoke, "Mister Sutton, do you have any more witn—"

Suddenly, Tibbitts spun in his chair, interrupting Judge Fogel. "Your honor!" he sputtered.

The gallery bustled at the commotion, and a wave of murmuring fell over the courtroom. Judge Fogel frowned deeply at Tibbitts. Cyrus dipped his head, and his eyes drew to slits as he glared across the aisle at the rooster.

"Your honor, the Animals have another witness!" said Tibbitts, almost breathless with excitement.

As one, the crowd let out a collective gasp followed by a cacophony of voices, some angry, others stammering excitedly.

"Objection, your honor!" howled Cyrus before Judge Fogel could even respond.

Judge Fogel never looked away from Tibbitts, conspicuously disgruntled at the late development. "Mister Tibbitts, the Animals have rested their case," he reprimanded Tibbitts. "You know well you may not call any further witnesses," he added, his voice barely audible above the bustling crowd.

Just as Tibbitts started to speak, Judge Fogel broke his gaze, the noise from the gallery finally creeping into his perception. He banged his hoof hard on the bench three times. "The courtroom will be silent!" he roared, his patience worn thin. With a handful of final whispers and murmurs, the gallery fell quiet.

Judge Fogel turned back toward Tibbitts and demanded harshly, "What is this all about, Mister Tibbitts?"

Tibbitts took a long gulp and looked down at the floor then slowly raised his head to meet eyes with Judge Fogel. "Your honor, the Animals acknowledge that we have rested our case," he said and then paused for a moment. "However, we offer an impeachment witness."

"Your honor," interrupted Cyrus curtly from the defense table, "Mister Tibbitts may not offer extrinsic evidence to impeach Mister Willis."

Tibbitts fired back, having regained his usual composure. "Your honor, the Animals are prepared to contradict Mister Willis' statement on direct that he *never harmed his animals*," he answered sharply. "Under the humans' Rules of Evidence, witness testimony is indeed allowed for purposes of impeachment if offered to contradict a factual assertion."

Judge Fogel furrowed his brow, considering the statement. Then he turned and looked toward Cyrus for a response.

"Your honor," responded Cyrus, sounding

exasperated, "any testimony alleging that Mister Willis has harmed *other* animals —as preposterous as such an allegation is — is clearly collateral to the matter at hand and is hardly admissible." Cyrus glanced at Tibbitts indignantly.

Judge Fogel turned back toward Tibbitts. "Mister Tibbitts, you know the humans' Rules of Evidence," he admonished. "Mister Sutton correctly states the law."

"Your honor," he started eagerly, "the proposed testimony does not involve *other* animals." He turned and looked Cyrus square in the eye. "The testimony is directly related to *the victim* in this case and is most certainly relevant." With the words, the crowd erupted. The humans in the gallery jeered and booed heartily.

"Sit down, rooster!" shouted a burly farmer from the edge of the crowd.

"Your turn is over, you stupid bird!" wailed a woman, the foul words belying her pleasant, polka dot dress.

"Kick him out!" howled another man.

Judge Fogel slammed his hoof once more against the bench, but the crowd continued to shout and curse. The old bailiff dog stepped forward aggressively from the back of the room. Judge Fogel again pounded his hoof on the bench. As the bailiff dog approached the rail to the gallery, he growled deeply and slowly, baring his long, white teeth. At the threat, the people slowly settled in their seats, and the courtroom grew quiet.

Judge Fogel turned back toward Tibbitts and considered him for a moment. "Mister Tibbitts, I will allow your impeachment witness, but if they do not testify directly to the matter at hand, this court will sanction you mightily for your behavior here today," he warned sternly.

"Thank you, your honor," said Tibbitts, nodding deferentially.

Across the aisle, Cyrus growled audibly from deep within his belly.

"You may call your witness," said Judge Fogel amidst the grumbling of the gallery.

CHAPTER 8

As the droning of the clock's hands ticked interminably, the courtroom grew deathly still with anticipation. On the balcony above, goats and chickens dipped their heads through the railing as if they might somehow impossibly catch a glimpse of the witness entering through the doors beneath them. The old bailiff dog had left several moments earlier, and the doors had long-since settled.

At the defense table, Cyrus and Willis turned fully in their chairs, staring restlessly at the door. Likewise, Tibbitts stood on his chair peering beyond the towering Holsteins, awaiting the entrance of his unexpected witness.

Then, one of the tall doors creaked and began to open slightly, the shrill sound like a sour trumpet in the vacuum of silence that engulfed the courtroom. Like a cresting wave, the crowd leaned forward, straining to see beyond the gap of the door. As if in response, the leathery black nose of the old bailiff dog poked through, and he leaned sideways against the door, holding it open, but he did not enter. The gaggle of farmers and workmen in the gallery craned their necks to see into the hallway, and a faint, impatient whispering began to rise within the crowd. Then, the bailiff dog entered and began walking down the aisle, and the door swung closed behind him. The murmuring and whispering grew louder as both sides of the gallery seemed perplexed at the delay in the witness' entry. Tibbitts began to pace in short circles in his chair in evident concern.

Just then, a Holstein on the aisle near the front row shrieked. "Ahhhhh!" she cried, her eyes wide with terror and focused downward near the short double doors leading to the well of the courtroom.

Suddenly, dozens of eyes — human and animal alike — swiveled toward the aisle, following the cow's gaze. Along the dull wooden planks, a chestnut brown mouse scurried along, his long pink tail trailing behind him like some ghastly worm. Audible gasps rose from either side of the gallery, and the balcony above followed suit. A fashionable woman in a fine, pillbox hat moaned loudly and fainted, slouching backward in the arms of a brawny laborer.

Undeterred by the commotion, the meager mouse hurried forward and slipped effortlessly under the space between the low double doors. As he scurried hastily between the prosecution and defense tables, Cyrus instinctively crouched low and leaned forward on his chair as if he might pounce. Just as the edges of his mouth raised into a gruesome hiss, the cat seemed to catch himself and settled back in the chair, glancing around to see if anyone had noticed, but the whole courtroom remained fixated on the tiny mouse. Even Tibbitts seemed startled at the commotion and sat rigid in his chair, watching the little rodent approach the witness stand. Only Judge Fogel seemed unperturbed as he reclined back in his chair emotionlessly and watched the scene unfold.

When the mouse reached the edge of the witness stand, he stopped and stood on his hind legs; his eyes searched up the towering table leg. His long teeth chattered anxiously, and his small, pink fingers spindled thoughtfully as he contemplated how to circumvent this obstacle. Just then, the old bailiff dog appeared behind him, lumbering to his side. The old dog lowered his head before the little mouse, and without hesitation, the mouse clambered onto the crown of the dog's head, grasping his way along the shaggy white hair. Then, the dog took one step forward and raised his head level to the table before the witness stand, pressing his nose against the wood. Without prompting, the little mouse scurried across his snout onto the slick wooden table and sat there, his tiny head swiveling left and right, digesting the scene around him.

In the gallery, the humans gaped slack-jawed, too stunned even to mutter their disbelief. Across the aisle, the animals whispered quietly among each other while the jury stared dumbfounded. Oblivious to it all, the little mouse perched there on his hind legs and twisted around to look at Judge Fogel, nodding quickly, as to acknowledge that he was ready to begin.

The white tufts above Judge Fogel's eyes rose briefly with restrained incredulity, and he nodded back, an almost imperceptible admiration for the plight of the small creature crept in to the gesture. Then, he delivered the oath, and in return, the mouse nodded feverishly, which proved enough for the moment.

Judge Fogel raised his head and cast it over the witness table toward Tibbitts. "Mister Tibbitts," he said, his tone more grave than usual, "I remind you once more of the scope of this testimony."

Tibbitts fluttered down from his chair. "Yes, your honor," he said as he landed and, in a fluid motion, drew his wings shut and began to pace across the well of the courtroom toward the jury box.

When he reached the railing before the jury, he turned toward the witness stand. "Good afternoon, sir."

The little mouse, still standing on his back legs, chattered and nodded quickly at the rooster. "Hello," he squeaked nervously; his voice was slight yet sharp. The crowd leaned forward to listen intently.

"Will you please state your name for the jury?"

The little mouse swiveled politely to face the jury. "I am Chauncey," he squeaked, his cadence and mannerisms distinctly odd.

Some of the jurors wrinkled their brows at the awkward creature. Tibbitts pressed onward, seeming somewhat hesitant about his new witness. "Mister Chauncey, can you please tell us why you're here today?"

The mouse chittered and turned back toward the gallery, his bulbous black eyes reflecting the last remnants of sun beyond the windows. "Something I saw," he chirped rather cryptically. There was muttering from the gallery, and Judge Fogel leaned forward impatiently in his chair.

Tibbitts glanced over the mouse and sensed Judge Fogel's brewing disposition at the late witness and hurried along. "You saw something relevant to why we are here today?"

"I did. Yes," said the little mouse hurriedly, the words rushing from his mouth as if he could barely contain them.

"Mister Chauncey, this *something* that you saw," he said, emphasizing the word, "did it occur on the defendant's' farm?" he asked, sweeping his right wing toward Willis.

The mouse responded with a bizarre urgency in his words, as if bursting with information yet unfamiliar with how to communicate except in short, choppy statements. "Indeed, indeed."

Judge Fogel leaned forward in his chair again, and this time, his eyes rose and met Tibbitts', an unspoken warning. Tibbitts continued, cutting quickly through any pleasantries. "Did you see Samuel Willis hurt an animal on his farm?"

At the question, the audience collectively inhaled and held their breaths, the air in the courtroom seemed to grow stagnant. Outside, the muted sound of warblers singing high in the magnolia just beyond the window pushed vainly through the plate glass windows.

"Indeed, I did," said the little mouse, his eyes affixed attentively on Tibbitts. The crowd exhaled in groans, mutters, and harsh whispers, clearly displeased. Judge Fogel looked up from the bench to the gallery, and the sounds subsided.

Tibbitts pushed forward. "Mister Chauncey, I

need you to explain in detail what you saw at the defendant's farm that day."

The little mouse knotted his pointy pink fingers together like a ball of yarn. His long brown and white whiskers flickered as his little mouth chewed anxiously. "Indeed," said the little mouse once more as he began to recount his tale.

As the last remnants of afternoon sun struggled through the wispy black tendrils adorning the thicket of trees near the creek's edge, Chauncey hurried through the tall grass toward the familiar red barn. His scavenging in the white clapboard house had been uneventful, and his belly grumbled mightily with hunger. As he darted along under cover of the grass, his mind raced as it always did with the thousand enemies that swarmed around him always — red-tailed hawks that circled the farm, the great, wandering animals with giant hooves, and even the stinging insects that assailed him with barbed tails, jabbing at his tender flesh. With his thoughts adrift among his fears, the little mouse pushed forward, seeking refuge in the shadows of the old barn.

Weeks ago, a quarrelsome owl had found its way into the barn and sat perched atop the highest rafter, scanning the piles of straw and mounds of debris for a furry meal. Chauncey had seen him there, watchful from the shadows, and it was not difficult to envision his broken carcass in the crook of the owl's wicked, curved beak. Since the intruder had taken occupancy in the old barn, Chauncey had not been back, yet as he hurried across the pasture, he longed to find that the dreadful creature long-departed.

Digging his tiny claws into the soft dirt, he headed straight for the small gap in the red wood and pressed his pointed nose inward then wriggled his tiny body quickly through the hole into the blackness of the barn. For a long moment, he stood perched on his hind legs, his tiny oval ears twisting forward and back, listening for sounds, while his bulbous black eyes scanned the darkness. When he was finally satisfied there was no threat, he scurried along the edge of the barn, headed toward the front where the farmer sometimes kept disheveled sacks of oats and barley. Just then, the wide doors swung open, and the sunlight shone into the barn like a luminous flare, casting a long square of light across the pale dirt floor. Instantly, Chauncey darted to his left into a large patch of straw and burrowed himself deep within, his heart pounding in his chest.

His ears perked as he could hear the old dog, Amos, slobbering and panting with his typical buffoonish excitement somewhere nearby. Then, he heard the rumbling of the hooves plodding drearily along the dirt, one by one, in their melancholy procession. All around him, the ground trembled, and stalks of straw quivered before him with each step. He peered his nose through a gap in the straw and saw them passing, the short line of Holsteins headed to the milking parlor. After the first one passed, Chauncey couldn't help but notice the second in line. Her legs wobbled shakily, and Chauncey's delicate nose could smell the sickness within her. She seemed to tremble unsteadily as she trudged valiantly onward into the parlor followed by the others.

To his left, Amos had entered the barn, loyally following the herd until he was sure they were all securely within the parlor. Then, Chauncey heard the soft thud of human footsteps in the dirt treading toward him, and a pair of tattered leather boots soon appeared to his left.

"Get on!" scowled an angry voice, and Chauncey saw a weathered hand reach down and swipe vainly at the old dog, shooing him away. The dog gave a quick, obedient yip and turned, gliding out of the barn. Then, the man lumbered forward into the milking parlor, breathing heavily in ragged, wheezing breaths.

Chauncey lost sight of him as he passed through the door of the parlor and entered the closest stalls. From the long shadows cast along the wall of the parlor, Chauncey could tell that the man had begun working his way along the row of cows. He could hear the clamorous clanking of the milking equipment as the man roughly attached the hoses. Occasionally, he heard a faint snorting from the cows, but largely, they remained silent. From where he sat hidden in the pile of straw, he could see the old cow in the second stall, still tottering left and right as if she might fall at any moment. The cow beside her occasionally turned her heard and looked at her ailing stall-mate, a sense of deep concern evident on her face.

After a moment, Chauncey could see the man's boots stepping briefly into the aisle and then moving into the stall with the ailing cow. The man crouched down below her and hoisted the milking equipment, attaching the rusted metal clamps to the old cow's nipples. Suddenly, the cow tottered and wobbled violently then fell toward the railing of the stall. Just as she did, the man dropped face-first to the ground and rolled into the aisle just as the cow fell hard against the metal bars dividing the stalls. A wave of anger swept across the man's bitter face as he rose to his feet. The cow righted herself and stood just as he charged into the stall and balled his fist, slamming it hard into her side. Her agonous groan filled the barn and pulsed through Chauncey's ears. Again, the old cow wobbled.

"You god damn better stand up straight!" roared the man, his voice laced with primal rage. The ailing cow tottered and wobbled before him again, her eyes blinking rapidly and her mouth gaped open, breathing heavily. The man glowered down at her sickly with his hands balled in tight fists by his side. Then, he stepped forward and grabbed the short rope of her halter and yanked her head violently backward, lines of spittle visible around his clenched teeth.

"Get on!" He pulled hard at the rope, forcing her toward him. The old cow stepped slowly backward as if the labored steps were literally draining the life from her. With each step, he jerked the rope again, pulling her violently backward until she stood in the aisle, sides heaving, then slowly, she turned back to face the entrance from the barn.

Chauncey sat silently in the straw, his eyes bulging with terror at the scene before him. His whiskers flittered nervously as he gazed on at the cruel dance between the old man and the cow. Beneath him, the ground began to rumble as the cow stepped one foot at a time slowly and methodically toward the door separating the milking parlor from the barn. Chauncey could see her approaching. The whites of her eyes shown wide, and her nostrils flared with arduous breaths. It was evident to the little mouse that she was fighting a battle within her mind just to stay on her feet.

The man stepped before her and yanked again on the rope, dragging her through the door. When she was halfway through, he stepped into the first barn stall and yanked again, pulling her from the aisle. She stepped forward again at his violent command, and as she did, her legs faltered. Her eyes gaped wide with terror, and she stepped forward desperately with her other foot, trying to regain her balance, but she failed. The old cow's legs buckled dramatically. As she did, the man took look one quick, loping step out of the way, bounding over the small pile of straw in which Chauncey hid, and the cow leaned forward violently and thundered into the hard dirt, halfway in the stall and half in the aisle, barely raising her head enough so her chin skidded across the ground. Finally, she came to a rest in a terrible heap, her legs splayed grotesquely around her.

Chauncey could hear the man standing there for a moment, breathing heavily. He could smell the rancid spittle dripping from his lips, laced with the fetid smells of meat and tobacco. He could feel the man's gaze falling ominously on the helpless cow, who lay just feet before him, her neck stretched along the ground and her front legs twisted helplessly behind her. She breathed heavily, and with each breath, the straw bristled and shifted around the little mouse, clearing a path between the two creatures.

In the shadows of the old red barn, their eyes connected — the helpless cow and the invisible mouse. The anguish in her eyes was unmistakable as she looked upon him helplessly, yet Chauncey could feel a small ripple of peace surge within her as her eyes met one of her own — two castoffs in the world of man. Chauncey's small, pink fingers spindled against each other feverishly as he stood there nervously, his beady eyes connecting inward with her broken soul.

Then, he heard the stoic trudging of the man as his feet pounded back to the milking parlor. His form cast a long shadow through the door of the parlor, and soon, he was gone. Once more, the barn fell quiet. Chauncey could see the man ahead in the distance, moving to the last stall and then crouching to fix the milking equipment to the last cow.

With the man safely out of sight, the little mouse lowered his gaze and stared ahead at the old cow before him. Her eyes wavered and grew small. Her breathing seemed to calm as she resigned herself to her predicament, seeking rest for her tired body. Chauncey wished he could dart from the pile of straw and help her, but he was much too small, and the task was much too large.

And so they sat there motionless in each other's presence for a long time. Beyond the doorway, the milking equipment clanked and rattled as the man moved from stall to stall, checking on the cows who stood impassively.

Before him, the downed cow's breathing slowed, growing controlled and steady. Her body sagged heavily into the hard dirt as if the floor of the old barn might consume her whole.

Chauncey poked his pinkish nose through the straw, his whiskers rattling the loose fibers around him. "Hello, ma'am," he started, awkwardly polite for such a moment. "How might I help you?" he asked, his voice quivering yet determined.

The old cow slowly rolled her eyes upward from the floor and stared despondently at the tiny mouse. A long breath exhaled through her nose, blowing a faint cloud of dust before her. Chauncey turned his head and coughed a short hack as the dust entered his nostrils. She simply lay before him in the dirt and said nothing.

He looked over her into the milking parlor and saw the long shadow of the man against the far wall. Slowly, he leaned forward and placed one of his tiny feet on the ground and then froze stiff, waiting for any movement or sounds of threat. Hearing none, he crept forward with the second foot and, once again, froze. He repeated this ritual with all four of his feet until he had fully emerged from the pile of straw. The cow looked on at this strange creature, her big black eyes following his bizarre movements. After a pause, he scuttled forward until he stood beside her long nose that lay flat against the hard ground. She swiveled her eyes downward at him until the whites shone brightly up against the rotted rafters where the barn owl perched hidden in the shadows.

Chauncey stood on his hind legs and rested his tiny hands on her nose and then started to run them frantically up and down the side of her fur, attempting to rouse her. The cow simply stared at him blankly, much too tired to stand or speak.

"Get up, you must!" squeaked the little mouse with all the urgency he could muster, scratching his claws feverishly up and down her nose. "Hurry, hurry!" he implored her.

But the cow simply stared at him. Her body could not rise, and she had not the energy to tell the little mouse, who nobly seemed to believe he could will her to stand.

"Up!" he pleaded with her, his voice now shrill and frenzied. He continued clawing at the side of her nose. Soon, his narrow sides began to expand and contract as the little mouse worked himself to exhaustion trying to rouse her. Once more, she expelled a great breath, and the dirt around her billowed, and the pile of straw fluttered. With this, the little mouse stopped, seeming to sense the unspoken response to his pleas.

Chauncey rested back on all fours before her, panting. He stood there just inches from her face, and once more, their eyes met in the shadows of the barn — hers hopeless and his afraid. After a moment, he turned and looked toward the milking parlor and began to tremble.

The din of clanking metal rose from the milking parlor as the man began unfastening the equipment from the cows. Before long, the sound of hooves thudding on the hard dirt filled the barn, and the wooden walls seemed to rattle as the cows, one by one, backed out of their stalls and began to take their positions in the aisle.

Chauncey looked once more at the cow before him, his eyes beseeching her one last time to rise. But, her eyelids drew heavy then she shut her eyes and lay there in the dirt. As the first cow loomed in the doorway of the milking parlor, Chauncey turned and darted back into the pile of straw, diving nose first into the debris.

One by one, the cows passed them, stepping carefully to the side of the downed cow as they exited the parlor and moved cautiously into the barn. As the last of the cows from the parlor entered, she paused momentarily at the downed cow and lowered her head, sniffing. Then, she let out a long, mournful bellow and stepped away quickly as the man scolded her with harsh words and a balled fist.

Slowly, the cows filed out of the barn followed by the man. Chauncey could hear the old dog at the entrance to the barn, his loud panting drowning out the pounding of hooves. Chauncey froze, listening for the dog to enter, prepared to dart through the gap in the barn wall if needed, but he never did. Soon, the man spoke brusquely, and the dog departed to herd the cows away.

For a long moment, the barn was silent and empty except for the lone cow and the tiny mouse. The last vestiges of sun filtered through the trees and shone in through the barn door, casting dancing shadows on the barren floor. In the distance, Chauncey could hear the cows moving further away, and he could hear the faint sounds of songbirds chirping from the woods near the creek.

Then, he heard two footsteps, and the barn doors began to close, the faint light receding into a pit of darkness, only the flickering electric lights from the milking parlor illuminating a long strip across the floor. For a long moment, the man stood motionless in calculating silence. Then, he began to approach. The little mouse tucked himself further into the straw as the sound of his footsteps drew ominously near.

Chauncey peeked through the straw and could see the man's worn boots standing before the pile of straw, looming above the sick cow. He stood there silently, his malignant stench permeating the tiny mouse's nostrils. Chauncey looked once more at the cow, who opened her eyes and stared straight ahead, connecting once more with his; never once did she gaze upward to acknowledge the man towering above her.

Then, Chauncey watched the man's feet step away out of view. He could hear the sounds of steel and wood clattering as the man searched for something in the far corner of the barn. Soon, the sounds stopped, and Chauncey could hear the man's feet thudding back across the barn — one step, then two, then three, then four, and now Chauncey could see him standing there in front of the pile of straw once more.

The fallen cow's eyes stared straight ahead at the little mouse, forlorn and lifeless, though she still breathed softly through her nose. Chauncey's heart raced as his senses tingled with danger all around him, but he dared not rush from the straw pile and be seen by the man.

And in his tiny, racing heart, he knew he must remain. For her.

Then suddenly above him, he heard the sharp rustle of fabric and felt a swift gust of wind as the man jerked his arms upward. Strands of straw fluttered and tumbled all around the little mouse.

"You ain't gonna do me no good like that," growled the man. Then, a sudden gust rushed downward into the pile of straw as heavy steel arced through the air and crashed into the cow's skull, the sickening sound reverberating through the barn. Blood red ribbons dashed in jagged streaks upon the rotted wooden walls.

Chauncey jerked upright in the pile of straw, and his eyes squeezed tight in terror. All around him, he could smell the man's putrid sweat, and when he opened his eyes, he saw the man's arms angled to the ground before him, the tendons of his leathery forearms pulsing beyond bony claws that clutched tightly to the end of an oaken axe handle, the blunt steel embedded gruesomely in the head of the cow. Chauncey's eyes bulged from his head in panic, and he looked upon her — her final gaze affixed upon him, now wide and dead. Around the edges of the sunken steel, blood seeped and ran in meandering streams through her black and white fur.

Grunting deeply, the man yanked upward on

the handle, drawing the blunt end of the axe from its grievous wound. Chauncey gaped in horror into the broken skull of the lifeless cow. As she lay there now, her body seemed even more splayed and twisted than before.

After a moment, he heard the man's footsteps, and once more, wood and steel clanked in the distance as the man dropped the axe back into the pile of tools. Then, the footsteps thudded toward the barn doors, pushing them open once more. The scant rays of afternoon sun seemed to wilt and fade just before the doors of the grim barn.

When Chauncey was sure the farmer had left, he darted from the straw pile toward the crack in the barn. As he fled, he could sense the watchful eyes of the barn owl upon him, yet he took no flight. After squeezing his way through the tiny opening, he scampered madly for the safety of the woods, carrying with him the horrors he had seen.

As the last words of Chauncey's tale faded into the cold silence of the courtroom, creatures of all sort — man and animal alike — sat awestruck. At the far end of the jury box, Tibbitts stood reverently, giving space to the little mouse. The jury — every one — sat wide-eyed and enthralled. After a moment, one of the chickens blinked rapidly as if waking from a stupor, and the goat gently bobbed back and forth, yet none broke their gaze from the witness.

Finally, after a long silence, Tibbitts lifted his head and looked to Judge Fogel. "The Animals have nothing further, your honor." With that, he returned quietly to the defense table.

Only when Tibbitts had settled into his seat did Cyrus leap down from his chair, his usual zeal noticeably absent. For a moment, he seemed to collect himself before slinking slowly across the floor toward the witness stand with his head down as if contemplating deeply.

In the background, the crowd finally began to rustle to life. Faint whispers passed throughout the wooden benches on either side.

"Mister Chauncey," started Cyrus bitterly, having mustered his usual disdain. The little mouse tittered on the wooden stand, staring down at the cat. "You come in to this courtroom with this...this," he said, feigning theatrically as if he struggled to find the word, "*fanciful* story that you expect us to believe."

The little mouse said nothing and merely stood on the witness stand, spindling his fingers together anxiously.

A brief hint of indignation crossed Cyrus' face at the mouse's lack of response. He tried again. "You expect that you can scurry from the usual filth of your kind into this courtroom and expect this courtroom to believe your tale?" Cyrus pressed in on the witness stand, his flaxen eyes leering at the mouse. "You expect that this jury," his left paw opened in a sweeping motion, "this *wise, prudent* jury, will take the word of a creature like you?"

Again, the little mouse was silent.

Tibbitts shifted in his seat but did not rise.

Cyrus inched even closer to the witness stand. The tips of his claws crept beyond the edge of his paws. "Sir, are you not quite literally a *rat*?" he snarled, his tone bitter and accusatory.

The animals gasped in the gallery. On the other side of the aisle, the humans nodded vigorously and began to jeer and mutter insults. The old bailiff dog stepped forward into the well of the courtroom, and Judge Fogel leaned forward in his chair and opened his mouth, preparing to silence the crowd.

Then, a gentle squeak cut through the cacophonous din. "I am a field mouse, sir," replied Chauncey politely, oblivious to the cat's insinuation.

In the gallery, some of the animals chuckled, while the humans sputtered and mumbled among themselves. Cyrus stared contentiously at the little creature for a moment then persisted with the examination.

"Sir," he said, patronizingly, "you did not have permission to be in the barn, did you?"

"I entered on my own," said the mouse, somewhat cryptically.

Cyrus sneered. "Samuel Willis did not grant you express consent to enter the barn, did he?"

"No consent, no, no," replied Chauncey.

"And this was not the first time you trespassed into the barn, was it?"

"I am in the barn many times," said the mouse. "Nice from the weather, it is," he added unprompted.

"In fact, Mister Chauncey, on many occasions, you have dug holes under the walls of the barn to facilitate your trespass, have you not?"

"I cannot dig through the wood," said the mouse, answering matter-of-factly. "But the dirt is soft."

Cyrus paused as if digesting the response and then continued. "And you have torn holes in bags of oats on numerous occasions and stolen property that did not belong to you?"

"Mice must eat." Chauncey spindled his tiny hands together once more.

Tibbitts hung his head, at a loss for any objection.

"So, Mister Chauncey, you have come before this court and admitted that you have trespassed.

You have admitted that you destroyed property. And you have admitted that you have stolen from Samuel Willis. Is that right?"

"These are human words," replied the little mouse. "These are not my words."

Cyrus ignored the response and forged ahead. "And although you are a trespasser, a thief, and a destroyer of property, you expect this jury to believe your incredible testimony here today?" he asked, turning to speak directly to the jury. "You ask this jury somehow to look past your continuous criminal behavior and your utter lack of credibility and accept that *you* — and only *you* — saw just what happened in that barn?"

"I say only what my eyes see," squeaked the mouse, still spindling his tiny hands.

Cyrus stared coldly at Chauncey. Behind him, the gallery was silent. For a long moment, the cat locked eyes with the mouse, and again, the latter stared back with his earnest, beady eyes, never looking away. Sensing his resolve, Cyrus turned to Judge Fogel. "No further questions, your honor."

CHAPTER 9

As Chauncey scuttled beneath the swinging double doors and hurried down the aisle, the sounds in the courtroom grew to a raucous din. On one side of the aisle, the humans bustled and babbled angrily with indignation at the mouse's testimony. As Chauncey hurried past, a burly farmer in dingy overalls spat at him, the dark, syrupy fluid landing just inches away from the mouse. The old bailiff dog glared at the man and bared his teeth ferociously but carried on ushering the mouse, feeling urgency to extract the witness from the courtroom.

On the other side of the aisle, the animals whispered feverishly among themselves. Goats turned to cows, and they spoke hurriedly in excited tones. Chickens squawked amongst themselves and flapped their wings restlessly. On the bench, Judge Fogel settled comfortably back in his chair, his eyes studying the crowd, sensing it best to let them expend their nervous energy before closing arguments.

After a moment, the old bailiff dog returned, re-entering the courtroom before the doors had even stopped swinging. He stopped in the aisle and turned toward the humans, his eyes resting on the burly farmer who had spat at the mouse. Again, he bared his teeth, and then a short, sharp bark pierced the courtroom, aimed directly at the culpable farmer. Slowly, the farmer lowered his head, and all around him, the crowd grew silent. On the other side of the aisle, the animals sensed the dog's patience wearing thin, and the clucking and neighing subsided rapidly. Soon, the courtroom fell into a familiar silence that had gripped the scene so often this day. Only then did the old bailiff dog turn and march back down the aisle, pushing his way through the low double doors and returning dutifully to his post beside Judge Fogel's bench.

Tibbitts and Cyrus sat properly in their chairs, backs to the audience, awaiting the next phase of the trial.

Judge Fogel remained reclined relatively casually in his chair, yet his coal-black eyes remained active, eyeing the courtroom until he was satisfied that all were settled. Then, he leaned forward and lowered his eyes intentionally to Cyrus. "Mister Sutton, do you have any further witnesses?"

Cyrus glanced almost imperceptibly at Tibbitts,

cutting his deep yellow eyes with unbridled disdain at his opponent. Then he turned back to Judge Fogel somewhat begrudgingly. "No, your honor, the defense rests." His words were unmistakably bitter. Behind him, the humans rustled in their seats apprehensively.

Judge Fogel turned toward Tibbitts. "Very well. We will now proceed to closing arguments." His tone bore a grave sense of finality. "Mister Tibbitts, are the Animals ready?"

Tibbitts cleared his throat, the burnt orange feathers on his broad breast bristling. "We are, your honor." His voice was filled with purpose.

"You may proceed," said Judge Fogel.

Tibbitts glanced down at his papers once more and then rose in his chair. As the afternoon light filtered through the long window onto the courtroom floor, Tibbitts seemed suddenly majestic. The red of his wattle shone brilliantly in the drab courtroom, and the bluish-green hue of his tail feathers cast an aura of sophistication against the plain wooden chair. Without lifting his wings, he lowered his body and hopped down off the chair, the faint clicking of his toes on the wooden floor the only sound. Then slowly, in measured paces, he walked toward the jury, his body smooth and controlled, absent the often sudden movements of which fowl of his type are prone.

Feet away, the jury settled as comfortably as they could into their chairs, bracing for these critical final moments. On one end, the red-faced turkey peered forward, his long neck almost stretching over the railing in anticipation of Tibbitt's argument. Beside him, the tawny brown goat stared bug-eyed, his black, horizontal pupils fixated on the approaching rooster.

"Good creatures of the jury," started Tibbitts, approaching to within feet of the jury box, "I want to begin by offering you my deepest appreciation for your most noble service here today." He inched even closer to the jury box, stretching his wings outward as if to encompass the entire jury. "Your duty here is indeed a most important one."

He lowered his head thoughtfully and began to pace down the length of the jury box then stopped and looked across the courtroom toward the defense table, his deep gaze falling on Willis. "The defendant sits before you today, accused of the crime of murder."

After a calculated pause, he continued. "Earlier today, he sat there before you," Tibbitts gestured toward the witness stand with one wing, "and wept openly as he told you what that farm meant to him . . . what the animals meant to him."

At the defense table, Willis straightened in his chair. He set his jaw, looking quite disconcerted at the attention, and then cast his eyes downward to the wooden floor.

"*This* defendant," continued Tibbitts, his tone rising to a mocking scoff, "would have you believe that, in the victim's hour of need, he was there by Ofelia's side, stroking her and comforting her as she lay on the hard dirt of that old red barn."

Tibbitts stepped away from the jury box and began to pace across the well of the courtroom, his burnt orange chest poked outward, his eyes cast to the floor. "*This* defendant would have you believe that Ofelia was but the victim of some cruel tragedy — the stray hoof of an errant cow, in his words."

Some of the jurors shifted in their seats as Tibbitts faced away from them, as if decorum demanded they only move when he faced away.

"But the defendant wasn't alone in his tale. Mister Bickers — the slaughter truck driver — testified to much the same today. He told you what an honorable, decent man the defendant is and how he always cared for his animals." Tibbitts reached the defense table and paused for a moment, looking once more toward Willis, who seemed to squirm in his chair under the rooster's gaze.

After a moment, Tibbitts turned and paced silently back to the jury. When he reached the edge of the jury box, he lifted his gaze and scanned the seven jurors. "I'm reminded of a story my momma told me when I was but a wee chick," he began, his tone becoming soft and casual.

"Before I found my way into the good town of Plum Grove, I spent my early days at a farm just past the railroad tracks." He lifted his head and gazed out the window for a moment as if remembering his childhood.

"That old farm sat at the edge of a great big stand of cottonwoods, and when I was but a little chick, my sisters and I used to roam all day in those woods, pecking at seeds from the flowers and digging in the moist soil for those big, fat worms that lived under the shade of those trees," he said, his eyes shifting longingly to the floor as if reliving the scene.

Then he looked up and scanned the length of the jury. "But when nighttime called, momma used to tell us to stay away from them trees and come roost in the open field. '*The shadows bring the foxes*,' she used to say."

Tibbitts turned slowly and faced Willis. "*The shadows bring the foxes*," he repeated, eyes affixed to the old farmer.

"And in the shadows of that old red barn on that fateful day, Ofelia couldn't walk to that open field. She was too tired, too sick, too broken," Tibbitts turned back to face the jury, and his eyes rested on the two chickens who returned his gaze intently, "and the fox came for her."

Wham! Tibbitts pounded his right wing against the rail of the jury box. The jurors shot upright in their seats, their eyes wide and startled.

"Samuel Willis," he said empathically, finally calling the man by name, "drove the flat end of that axe into Ofelia's skull while she lay there helplessly before him because she was wasn't worth a thing to him anymore!"

Tibbitts stared at them silently for a moment, allowing the words to linger. Then he turned away from the jury, and as one, collectively, they seemed to exhale. He took a few steps into the well of the courtroom and turned to face them once more. "But there was something else in the shadows of the barn that Samuel Willis didn't count on," he said and then paused for a moment, "the *truth*."

"While Samuel Willis stood over Ofelia and bashed her skull in with that axe, he wasn't alone. Down there in that pile of straw, someone was watching, and he came here today and told you exactly what he saw," said Tibbitts as he gestured toward the empty witness stand.

Behind the witness stand, Judge Fogel sat reclined in his chair watching Tibbitts intensely.

"We don't need to wonder what happened in those shadows, good creatures of the jury. Mister Chauncey came here today and sat there before you to tell you *exactly* what happened."

Tibbitts continued, his tone rising. "But my worthy opponent," he said, waving a wing toward Cyrus, "will no doubt come up here and tell you that the mouse never saw a thing. He'll tell you that Mister Chauncey is a thief, a scoundrel, and should not be believed."

Once more, Tibbitts walked toward the jury. "But should you also not believe Miss Geraldine, the last cow to leave the milking parlor – the last creature to see Miss Ophelia alive?"

"She took this stand and told you that Ofelia was sick that day — 'milk fever' they called it." His disgust in the words was palpable. "Sick and exhausted from years of labor on the defendant's farm, she was forced into the milking parlor that day just like every other day."

"But on this day, she could barely stand. You heard Miss Geraldine testify that Ofelia tottered and almost fell over," he continued. "She testified that Samuel Willis rose and punched her hard in the side. Instead of treating her, comforting her, or caring for her like he claims, he balled his fist tight and slammed it hard into her side." Again, Tibbitts slammed his wing down on the rail of the jury box, and once more, the jurors startled back in their seats.

"But that punch to the side was only a sign of the grim things to come," he said. "Miss Geraldine told you how Samuel Willis dragged Ofelia by a rope from that milking parlor and pulled her into the barn. She staggered and stumbled along the way, barely able to carry her own weight."

Tibbitts walked toward the end of the jury box where the turkey and goat looked on enraptured. Throughout the courtroom, the gallery sat silently, listening to his every word. On the bench, Judge Fogel pressed his front hooves together before him thoughtfully.

"Finally, Ofelia could walk no more, and she wobbled and fell there, halfway in the stall. And *that*, members of the jury, is where she would die," he added, the last word unmistakably poignant. He turned and looked at Willis. "There in that hard dirt, just before the ever-so-important pile of straw, she met the cold steel of Samuel Willis' axe."

"You heard Miss Geraldine testify that she walked past Ofelia on her way out of the milking parlor. You heard her tell you how the cows stepped gingerly around their fallen friend and how she leaned down and comforted Ofelia before Samuel Willis dragged her along."

Tibbitts lowered his head in thought and paced slowly down the length of the jury box, the silence enveloping him. Then he turned and raised his head. "Then, you heard from Mister Amos, the loyal dog of Samuel Willis," he said, "a dog so loyal he served a man who repeatedly kicked and yelled at him."

"But *this* . . . *this* was simply too much," he added as he set his eyes upon the old Suffolk sheep in the jury box. "Even a loyal old farm dog has his limits."

"Mister Amos told you how he approached the barn that day, rushing up from the creek in time for the cows to be herded back to the corral. He told you how he heard whimpering through the walls of that old red barn. He told you how he heard the sickening, deathly thud of something blunt and the pained groan that followed. And he told you how ten cows entered and only nine made it out."

Tibbitts turned and paced back down the length of the jury box. "That old dog heard his master kill Ofelia, and it sickened him so much that he couldn't keep the secret anymore."

At the defense table, Cyrus let out an audible sign, feigning boredom at the closing.

"But that's not all!" he bellowed sharply, as if responding to Cyrus' indignation. Tibbitts raised both of his wings in the air dramatically. "Indeed, there is more!"

The humans bristled in their seats and grumbled in disdain at the old rooster.

"Yet one more of Samuel Willis' loyal servants came before you to testify," he said. "Mister Horace — Samuel Willis' donkey, who had begrudgingly plowed those fields for decades — took the stand and described the conversation he had with the defendant the very next day."

"Mister Horace came here and told you what the defendant said to him in a fit of rage," said Tibbitts. "*'You gonna make me do to you what I did to that old heifer?'*"

He repeated the words, his tone rising. "*'You gonna make me do to you what I did to that old heifer?'*" Tibbitts' yellow eyes scanned up and down the jury box, ablaze with passion.

Willis shifted uneasily in his chair. Behind him, the humans sat stone-faced as they listened indignantly to the bellicose rooster, who preened up and down the length of the jury box, claws clicking across the old hardwood.

He turned to face the jury once more. "Ofelia died in the shadows of that old red barn at the blunt end of Samuel Willis' axe, her skull crushed and her blood seeping into the ground," Tibbitts continued. "Murdered simply because she could produce no more. Murdered because she was worth nothing to Samuel Willis. Murdered because she was just an animal, and her life meant just as much to Samuel Willis as the dirt on which she died."

Tibbitts stood before them, wings clasped behind his back. His eyes scanned the jury, looking each member in the eye. Each looked back at him nervously.

"My momma told me that the shadows bring the foxes," he said, his words growing soft and low, drawing the audience inward.

He turned from the jury and paced one final time across the well of the courtroom, head bowed. For a long moment, he stood there in silence. Finally, he lifted his gaze, and his eyes slowly scanned the gallery. Then he turned and walked back toward the jury.

"But even the darkest shadows can't hide the truth," he said, his voice resolute. "And the undeniable truth is that, on September 2nd in that old red barn, Samuel Willis retrieved an axe, and he drove it into Ofelia's skull while she lay helpless in the dirt. This, members of the jury, is the truth." His eyes scanned them one more time. "And for this truth, I ask you to find Samuel Willis guilty of the crime of murder."

With that, he turned and walked slowly back

to the defense table to a hushed courtroom. When he reached his chair, he fluttered his wings ever-so-briefly, landed gently in the chair, and settled to rest.

Across the aisle, Cyrus sat motionless in his chair, his eyes digesting the contents of his papers one last time. Judge Fogel peered out at the crowd in the gallery watchfully, and then his eyes shifted down and rested on Cyrus. The cat sensed his gaze, inhaled deeply, then leapt gracefully down from the chair.

With the air of a stalking wildcat, he slinked toward the jury, his form low and his belly just inches above the ground. As he neared the jury box, he stopped his prowl and rested slowly back on his haunches before them.

His words were soft and gentle at first, the wily cat adopting a subdued approach. "Members of the jury," he started, "today, you have sat patiently and listened to the day's testimony. You have heard the witnesses, and you have seen the full cases presented."

"And despite all you have witnessed here today, through these many witnesses and these hours of testimony, it all boils down to a single word." His voice was pleasant, and his deep yellow eyes studied the jury from one end to the other. He paused for a moment.

"*Vengeance*," he said with a sudden hint of bit-terness, letting the word hang openly in the court-room.

"*Vengeance*," he said once more and sat there in silence. Faint, agreeable mutterings rose within the gallery of humans.

"What you have heard here today is not about justice, my good creatures," he added, still scan-ning the jury. "Make no mistake!" he said, his voice suddenly rising to a crescendo. "Not once to-day has the defense argued that Samuel Willis was not a farmer. Not once have we told you that Sam-uel Willis did not make his living on the backs of animals. And not once did we tell you that Samuel Willis did not follow *the old ways*," he added, enunciating the final words.

"But my friends," he rose from his haunches and walked even closer to the jury box, "the old ways are not on trial here today." In the gallery, several humans grumbled audibly in vigorous agreement.

"As we sit here today, things are quite differ-ent. The animals are *free*," he said, pandering the jury with the drawn out word. "Free to live their lives with liberty, and dignity, and freedom from the chains of man."

In the jury box, the goat nodded instinctively in agreement with Cyrus.

"But on the day in question, things were not this way," he continued. "On the day in question, the animals were still bound by their chains, and though Samuel Willis knows now the injustice of the old ways," with his paw, Cyrus gestured toward Willis sitting somberly at the defense table, "you must not punish him simply for the old ways."

"Samuel Willis is not here before you because he partook in the old ways. Samuel Willis is here before you charged with a single act —the killing of Miss Ofelia." Cyrus began to pace down the length of the jury box. As one, the juror's eyes followed him until he reached the far end before the bald-headed turkey. He turned toward them once more.

"And it is only *this charge* that you must decide here today," he implored them. "But make no mistake that Mister Tibbitts wishes you to punish Samuel Willis for the old ways." Tibbitts lowered his head as if not to dignify the statement.

"As he stood here before you today, Mister Tibbitts tried admirably to seed your anger with tales of the old ways. He paraded you with witnesses who recounted one sad tale after another. But when it comes to the one true charge against Samuel Willis . . . Mister Tibbitts offered you very little indeed," he added, lowering his tone to a near whisper as he shook his head slightly from side to side.

Cyrus turned and slinked into the well of the courtroom. When he neared Tibbitts' table, he paused and turned to face the jury once more. "When this trial began," he started, his voice rising, "the burden of proof rested here with Mister Tibbitts." Theatrically, he rested his paw on the leg of the table.

For several seconds, he stood there silently. Across the courtroom, the jurors studied him intensely. The snow white duck looked on attentively, his bright orange beak gaping slack jawed while, behind him, the mottled pig gazed keenly with her deep, coal-black eyes.

"And here, the burden remains," added Cyrus, his tone laced with a hint of finality.

Tibbitts stared impassively over the table at the cat, plainly refusing to engage in the display.

Cyrus approached the jury box again. "Members of the jury, I implore you to ask yourselves — what has Mister Tibbitts offered today to prove that Samuel Willis is guilty of the actual crime for which he has been charged?" The cat peered closely into the eyes of each juror.

"I'll tell you what he's brought you!" he bellowed.

"First, he brought you Miss Geraldine, who

most conveniently was the last creature ever to see the victim alive," he ranted. "But Melvin Bickers sat right here," he gestured to the witness stand, "and told you that he saw clear and unmistakable hoof marks . . . *hoof marks* on the victim's skull."

Cyrus again paced to the end of the jury box and stood over the rail before the turkey and the goat. He cast his eyes down the length of the jury and continued.

"Then, Mister Tibbitts paraded Samuel Willis' senile old dog up here before you. The same old dog who was often late to move the herd because he was too deaf to hear the calls for him to come." Cyrus' voice was full of venom. "The same old dog who sat here before you nervously, fidgeting, and struggling to maintain the story that Mister Tibbitts had fed to him. The same old dog who was so blind he couldn't even identify a man wearing glasses just rows away from him!" Cyrus jabbed his paw toward the gallery.

Then, his voice lowered. "The same old dog who could have run away across that creek at any time, but stayed with Samuel Willis for years and years," he said, leaning forward into the jury box, "because he knew what kind of man Samuel Willis was — good man, a decent man, a hardworking man who took care of his animals. And that's why that dog never left his side."

Cyrus stood and walked to the far end of the jury where the Suffolk sheep and the duck sat. They looked anxious as the cat slinked near and sat before them.

"And then, at the very last minute, when Mister Tibbitts' case is crumbling, a secret witness reveals himself," he said derisively. "Mister Tibbitts would have you believe that Mister Chauncey is some bringer of truth, some shining light through the dark clouds of doubt."

Cyrus scoffed. "But far from it, good creatures. Mister Chauncey is nothing more than a ruse destined to save the prosecution's crumbling case. Who better to claim they witnessed what happened in that barn than a tiny mouse that no one could see, no one could verify was actually in that barn."

He turned and faced Tibbitts, speaking to him directly. Tibbitts returned his gaze. "At the very last minute, Mister Tibbitts springs upon us what he feels is the perfect witness, someone so small, so unnoticeable that his story cannot possibly be refuted."

"But members of the jury, you know better than to believe the mouse," he said as if speaking a universal truth. "You know better than to believe the lowliest of creatures who scampers around beneath our feet, belly dragging in the filth and dirt, beady eyes endlessly searching to steal, thieve, and pillage. Mister Tibbitts could not have conjured a more ignoble creature to stand before you and purport to share *the truth*," he said mockingly to Tibbitts.

Cyrus turned back toward the jury. All around, the humans and animals sat silently, enraptured by the cat's performance.

"Members of the jury, when the lies and emotions of Mister Tibbitts' case are stripped bare, when the vengeance he seeks for the old ways is set aside, when you move beyond the biases of Mister Tibbitt's witnesses, their disabilities in hearing, sight, and integrity . . . you are left with a very simple truth indeed."

Cyrus' eyes swept slowly back and forth across the jury. "On September 2nd, Samuel Willis went about his day like every other farmer in Plum Grove, moving the cows to the milking parlor for a good day's work. And when he saw that one of his cows, Miss Ofelia, was ill that day, he moved her as he always did to the stall so that she might recover. But she never made it to that stall; her legs buckled beneath her, and she fell halfway into the aisle," he said, glancing down as if conjuring the aisle of the old red barn.

"And so he let her rest there while he finished the milking. And when they were done, Samuel

Willis carefully paraded the remaining cows out of the parlor and through the barn. But on that day, fate intervened. With Samuel Willis at the head of the herd, the last Holstein stumbled and pressed her legs out to find her footing, and one of those legs crashed into the skull of Miss Ofelia, killing her where she lay there on that barn floor," he said, gesturing down with his paw.

His eyes narrowed thoughtfully. "Members of the jury, sometimes the truth is simple. Sometimes the truth does not require complicated stories or obfuscations. Sometimes the truth is right there in front of you."

He rested his paw on a vertical rail of the jury box. "Today, the truth is right here before you. And I ask you not to be fooled by the false words that Mister Tibbitts has offered you today. I ask you not to fall victim to the urge for vengeance as he wishes you to do," he said to them as he gestured toward Tibbitts with a flippant wave of his paw. "I ask only that you look beyond the misdirection and find the simple truth. And when you find it, I ask you to acquit Samuel Willis. This *is*," he drew out the word, "what justice demands."

With that, he turned and paced slowly back to the defense table, where Willis sat attentively, anxiously awaiting his return. As Cyrus leapt gracefully from the floor into his seat, the old man lowered his head in a deep nod of appreciation.

CHAPTER 10

J udge Fogel leaned forward in his seat as the bustle of the gallery faded into an anticipatory silence. His pinkish nose twitched and ever-vigilant, his wide eyes surveyed the courtroom from one side to the other. A short distance away, the jurors fidgeted nervously in their seats, sensing the focus would now turn to them.

"Members of the jury," began Judge Fogel in his deep baritone, turning in his chair to face them, "you have now heard testimony from both sides."

At the end of the jury box, the turkey warbled softly. Nearby, the pig fidgeted and panted anxiously.

"Now, the turn is yours." His voice was deep and clear as he rested the ultimate responsibility upon the seven animals gathered before him. "In a moment, I will ask that you leave the courtroom and return to the jury chambers, where you will begin your deliberation."

Willis bowed his head. Beyond the tall windows, the dying sun cast its waning light through the dusty panes and drew a long shadow across the defense table. In the gallery, the humans stirred, apprehensive at the looming verdict. A sturdy young man in the front row stretched over the railing and patted Willis on the back. The old farmer did not respond.

"When you return to this courtroom, you will be asked for your verdict on the charge —one count of murder," instructed Judge Fogel. With the last word, a weighty cloud seemed to settle over the courtroom, and the air grew tense and still.

"You are to consider only the evidence presented before you today. You must not consider any biases, emotions, or other information that was not presented to you at trial," he admonished. Several humans grumbled indignantly at the pending judgment of their fellow man by a haggard pack of farm animals.

"I will now appoint a foreperson, whose job it will be to communicate the verdict from the jury once you have concluded your deliberations," added Judge Fogel.

In the jury box, the jurors squirmed. The white duck seemed to lower his head so as not to be selected. Nearby, the sheep averted his eyes from his fellow species behind the bench. The two chickens anxiously rustled their wings and bobbed their heads in awkward circles.

Judge Fogel peered out at the jury. "Juror Number One," he declared, his eyes falling on the long-necked turkey, who peered nervously around the courtroom. His eyes grew wide at the words. "You have been selected as the foreperson, whose duty it is to report the verdict to this court-room. Do you understand?"

The turkey warbled loudly. His head swiveled around at the other jurors as if he might somehow relinquish the responsibility. Their eyes turned away as he looked upon them. Finally, he turned back to Judge Fogel. "Yes," he said, his voice quiv-ering.

Judge Fogel scanned the jury shrewdly. "Very well, then," he said and glanced toward the old bailiff dog. "You may now return to the jury room."

The brown goat was on his hooves before any of them, seemingly eager to leave the oppressive environs of the courtroom. One by one, they rose from their seats as tufts of fur and feathers wafted slowly to the courtroom floor. Led by the sheep at the far end of the jury box, they stepped forward with hooves and claws clattering on the wooden floor, then turned sharply around the railing and headed for the rear door. There, the old bailiff dog waited for them, bracing the door open on his broad shoulder.

In a disorderly procession, they filed out of the courtroom as dozens of eyes stared hard into their backs. When they were gone, the door swung shut, and the old bailiff dog returned to stand beside Judge Fogel's bench. The judge scanned the gallery once more as if making sure none had dared exit before him and then rose, his black robes loosening and sagging down across his wooly frame. Without a further look at the gallery, he hopped down from the far side of the bench and pushed his way through the other door and disappeared.

"Court is adjourned," bellowed the old bailiff dog to the crowd, and at once, they stood and began buzzing excitedly amongst themselves, the voices of humans and animals merging into a discordant stew.

The animals seemed to hesitate before departing, clearly sensing the overt hostility of the humans. Eventually, the gaggle of dusty farmers and their women in the bright floral prints and polka dot blouses started to shuffle out from their seats, casting looks of dispersion on the animals, who huddled and chattered among themselves. As the humans passed down the aisle, they hurled insults and profanities under their breaths at the animals, who looked fearful but did their best to ignore the taunts. The old bailiff dog moved forward a few paces, ready to act should the need arise. Eventually, the humans all exited the courtroom and moved into the broad hallway.

Then, one by one, the animals moved from their benches and shuffled into the aisle. The old Holsteins led the way, followed by the thudding of pig's hooves, the clacking of chicken's claws, and the soft thump of tiny rabbit feet.

The hallway of the courtroom was a raucous scene. Down the hall to the right, near the front door to the courthouse, the humans gathered. The wide doors were held open by a pair of men smoking cigarettes, and the humans streamed and milled in and out of the courthouse at leisure. To the left of the courtroom, the animals gathered in a huddle, continuing their fevered conversations. Many of the Holsteins gathered around Geraldine, who had waited in the hall with the other witnesses during the trial but now stood in a comforting half-circle of her fellow kind. Beside her, Horace rested on his haunches, looking quite exhausted from the day's events.

Sensing his dismay, a cottony, black and white rabbit hopped across the hallway and nuzzled his pink nose into Horace's fur, offering comfort. He reacted little and simply stared off into the space of the bustling hallway; the old donkey wasn't long for this world.

Unseen in the shadows beneath a wilting wooden chair on which a pair of threadbare chickens roosted, Chauncey sat alone, his anxious eyes scanning the hooves and claws around him for any signs of danger. As the creatures buzzed around him, no one seemed to notice the little mouse.

"Thank you, Geraldine," said one of the Holsteins earnestly. "Thank you for what you have done today." The Holstein nodded with deep appreciation. Around them, there were indistinct mutters of agreement from the others. "And thank you, Horace," added the Holstein, glancing down at the old donkey, who barely mustered a slight nod.

There was graveness in the air around the animals as they gathered in the hallway and awaited the verdict.

"I did what must be done," said Geraldine somewhat glumly.

Down the hall, the humans whispered and muttered among themselves, their words harsh and their eyes often casting angry looks at the animals gathered at the far end of the corridor. After a few moments, the old bailiff dog entered the hallway from the courtroom, his eyes searching the crowd, seemingly satisfied at the distance between the two groups.

For a long time, he stood there at the doorway like a sentinel. The humans, respectful of his presence, averted their eyes from the animals and kept their bitter words to themselves.

For a long time, they stood in their collective groups inside the courthouse hallway as the sun set low on the horizon and darkness filtered through the windows. The electric bulbs of the old courthouse lights crackled and buzzed, casting a drab, yellowish light on the plain beige walls. On their end of the hallway, the animals lay on the ground, resting in groups, some with heads on the sides of others. The chickens had wasted no time roosting on the windowsills and railings of the scant chairs that dotted the space.

At the other end of the hall, the humans stood or sat on the floor. Those sitting leaned against the wall, some with legs crossed and others extended into the hallway. Others dozed as their objectionable snores echoed down the hallway to the ears of the animals.

Soon, the whole hallway grew quiet save for the soft sounds of slumber of man and animal alike. For hours, they rested like this in a weary truce as night lay across the fields and woods beyond the courthouse window.

Then, the soft pitter patter of feet echoed on

the checkered floor, and the distant sounds drew near the animals. As one, they awoke with wide eyes, sensing a threat.

From the far end of the courthouse hallway, a small boy approached, his sparkling blue eyes shone beneath heavy eyelids. Clad in dusty overalls with cornstalk hair, he crept toward the animals as quietly as he could.

The chickens rustled on their roosts, and the rabbits pressed against the wall, seeking someplace to hide. Dutifully, Horace rose to protect them, his rigid joints bending audibly in the quiet of the hallway. He lumbered forward to meet the interloper. Behind him, the Holsteins stared nervously.

There in the hallway beneath the flickering lights of the Plum Grove Courthouse, the old donkey met the little boy.

Respectfully, the boy stopped several paces before Horace and lowered his head. Then quietly, he spoke, his voice instilled with the purity of youth. "I just wanted to say," he stammered slowly, "that I'm sorry."

All around him, the animals seemed to soften as the tension fell from their tired bodies. The wary gazes of narrowed, dubious eyes turned to thoughtful expressions as they studied the boy. On the windowsill, the chickens settled back to their roosts.

"I'm sorry for what we done to you," the boy added, his voice barely more than a whisper. And with that, he simply turned and walked back down the hallway toward the humans, his small feet treading gently into the distance.

For another hour, the humans and animals sat motionless in the hallway. The quiet of the courthouse was punctuated only occasionally by abrupt snores and the occasional rustling of wings as a chicken or turkey sought comfort on a makeshift perch.

Suddenly, the door to the courtroom flung open; the shrill creaking of the tired hinges pierced the silence. The old bailiff dog padded out from the courtroom, his head swiveling left and right, assessing the scene.

"The jury has reached a verdict!" he bellowed, rousing any who lingered in sleep.

At once, the air in the hallway grew charged with the nervous tension that had given way hours before to sheer exhaustion. Hurriedly, the groggy animals and humans pushed themselves upward on arms, wings, and hooves and rose from the floor.

The humans grumbled and whispered among each other, speaking in the wary tones of those who expected an unfavorable verdict. Down the hallway, the animals waited nervously yet sub-dued, huddling together in the corner and conceding first entry to the humans.

As they shuffled past, several old farmers and tired workmen cast scornful glances to the animals. Men and women clutched hands with the few yawning children with their heavy eyes. One by one, they began to take their seats on the wooden benches.

When the humans passed and the great double doors swung shut, the animals began to move as a herd with the old donkey, Horace, leading the way. Slowly, they proceeded, webbed feet shuffling along behind great hooves. Behind them, Amos appeared as if from nowhere and mingled in nervously with the crowd, unsure how he would be received. Yet, there was nary an objection as he slid his way into the throng that moved as a collective mass of feather and fur.

As the animals took their seats, the old bailiff dog stood at the center of the courtroom, keeping order over the procession. Just as the doors began to close, Chauncey slipped through the crack and scurried into the courtroom. On the human side, a small boy gasped loudly at the sight of the rodent and raised his hand to his mouth in horror.

As he watched Chauncey approach, Horace lowered his snout to the ground. The little mouse turned toward him, somewhat surprised. But without much hesitation, he scuttled up Horace's snout and across the crown of his head. The old donkey stepped backward until he was flush against the courtroom wall and then dropped unceremoniously to his haunches. Chauncey circled on the top of his head while Horace rolled his eyes upward at the unseen creature. After a moment, the mouse settled on a comfortable spot and rested back on his hind legs, perched high enough to see the proceedings.

When the crowd had settled, the old bailiff dog's commanding voice filled the courtroom. "All rise!"

And they did. As one, the humans and animals rose. Horace's legs buckled slightly as he stood, and the little mouse held on tightly to a tuft of gray-brown fur. In the row just ahead, Amos rose to all fours, dipping his head to peer through the wall of Holsteins before him.

Then, the rear door of the courtroom opened, and Judge Fogel's beady eyes flickered like stones of onyx in the glimmer of electric light beyond in the corridor. He emerged stoically, his demeanor grave and ceremonial. His eyes surveyed the courtroom for a moment, and then he stepped purposefully to the bench, resting his front hooves on the chair, and leapt forward. The old bailiff dog approached and clenched the end of Judge Fogel's robe in his teeth, pulling the rumpled fabric free from beneath the Judge's hooves and straightening it. Judge Fogel turned and nodded slightly to the dog in appreciation.

Then, he turned and gazed out into the gallery. The room grew deathly silent. Beyond the tall windows, the shrill screech of a distant barn owl echoed in the starless night. From the balcony above, a soft wisp of fur fluttered down. The eyes of the courtroom followed hypnotically as it drifted lazily and landed gently on the wooden floor.

When it finally came to rest, Judge Fogel spoke. "You may bring in the jury."

Without hesitation, the old bailiff dog turned and exited through the rear door. A moment later, he returned, leading the seven jurors to their seats. Once more, the turkey led the way, his eyes nervously darting about the courtroom. The brown goat, chickens, pig, duck, and sheep followed close behind, each avoiding eye contact with the gallery.

When they were properly in their seats, Judge Fogel turned in his chair. "Foreman," he said, his brow seeming to furrow as he recognized the awkwardness of the word, "has the jury reached a verdict?"

The turkey turned, his eyes bulging, and looked down the seats at his fellow jurors as if seeking validation. Once more, they simply stared ahead at the wooden floor. His face flushed bright red as he turned back to Judge Fogel. "Yes, your honor," he warbled unsteadily.

"Very well," replied Judge Fogel. Once more, his eyes absorbed the crowd. Humans and animals alike stared ahead, some fixated on the turkey, others blankly returning Judge Fogel's gaze. He continued without hesitation. "On Count One, the murder of Miss Ofelia, how does the jury find?"

The air seemed to suck from the room, leaving a hollow stillness in its place. Dozens of eyes bored straight through the turkey, whose snood drew short before his crimson face. As he stood there in silence, his breast slumped and his long neck quivered, causing his wattle to tremble. But then, as if resolving himself to the moment, he stood upright, his body welling with pride.

Slowly, his pale beak opened, and he began to speak. "The jury finds the defendant, Mister Samuel Willis . . . *guilty* of the murder of Miss Ofelia."

As the words left his beak, a great commotion erupted from the humans. Throughout the gallery, profanities and words of aggression spilled into the courtroom. The soles of leather boots squeaked loudly on the wooden floor as they stood or twisted in their seats, sharing looks of disbelief and utter disgust.

Before them, Willis slumped at the defense table, his shoulders sagging dramatically and his body seeming to crumble like a broken marionette. He wilted forward and buried his head in his arms. Next to him, Cyrus turned slightly toward the jury, his disdain barely veiled behind thinly drawn eyes.

At the prosecution table, Tibbitts, as usual, was emotionless and only stared straight ahead to the back wall of the courtroom. The rooster appeared to take little joy in sending a man — even a man like Willis — to the gallows.

Behind him, the animals whispered excitedly amongst each other, their jubilation guarded with darting, nervous eyes cast toward the humans, ever-alert for the formation of a mob. Only small peeps and chortles of joy arose from the group in tempered celebration.

Judge Fogel banged his hoof on the bench. "There will be order in the courtroom!" he bellowed, his voice booming off the unadorned walls. Shortly, the boisterous buzzing subsided to a muted hum, and the humans begrudgingly began to retake their seats. At the defense table, Willis remained with his head down and motionless.

"Thank you," said Judge Fogel as he nodded to the turkey and then turned back to the courtroom. His eyes fell on Willis. "Samuel Willis," he commanded, letting let the words hang in the stagnant air of the courtroom.

When Willis failed to acknowledge, Cyrus leaned over him and lowered his head, whispering something in his ear. Then slowly, the old farmer lifted his head from his arms and straightened his shoulders. He glowered back at Judge Fogel, his face bearing an insolent scowl like an ugly scar.

Judge Fogel returned the gaze unemotionally. "The jury has found you guilty in the murder of Miss Ofelia."

Willis' lips pursed and twisted as if foul words might spew forth. Yet, he remained silent.

Judge Fogel continued. "This court will now sentence you for the crime of murder."

Once more, the humans grumbled angrily in the gallery. Through the tall windows, the silver rays of moonlight pressed into the courtroom, seeming to usurp the warm glow of the electric light. Long shadows stretched across the wooden floor. In the jury box, several of the animals inhaled deeply, as if bracing themselves for the moment of condemnation.

Perched atop his bench, Judge Fogel's eyes

rose slightly to the gallery at the commotion and then returned to the defendant before him. "Before the court sentences you, you may have an opportunity to speak, if you so wish."

Willis's eyes averted from Judge Fogel, and he stared straight ahead for a long moment. Beside him, the gray cat looked stoically down at the table with nothing to offer in the moment. Then, Willis braced his weathered hands on the wooden armrests of his chair and thrust himself upright, his once-feeble form seeming to regain strength in these final moments. As he stood, his back straightened, and he turned slightly to face the gallery of animals, his countenance still bitter.

He opened his mouth to speak then hesitated. His eyes looked upon the animals full of spite. Then once more, his narrow lips parted and he spoke. "I been on that land all my life," he said and then paused. "That land and them animals, they're all I ever knew."

In the gallery of animals, dozens of eyes stared back at him. Neither feather nor fur bristled as the animals gazed resolutely at the old farmer.

Then, he turned toward the humans in the gallery. His chest seemed to swell with pride, and his shoulders lifted. Standing there framed in the long shadows that fell around him, he no longer looked like the downtrodden defendant from hours before but stood now as the martyr of the old ways.

In the gallery, the humans looked upon him affectionately. Throughout the benches, heads nodded and faint words of encouragement spilled from the lips of man and woman alike.

Willis turned toward the animals, and his face steeled. "I lived my life by the old ways." His thin lips twisted downward into bitter sneer. "And I ain't one bit sorry for it," he spat. "If the old ways is dead . . . I'll die right along with 'em." He glared coldly at the Holsteins in the front row and, without another word, turned his back to them and settled into his seat.

High above on the bench, Judge Fogel peered down at the defense table, his expression indiscernible. "Samuel Willis," he began, his voice cold and formal, "this court is prepared to impose judgement on you today." He leaned forward and pressed his front hooves together thoughtfully upon the bench. "This jury has found you guilty of the murder of Miss Ofelia. Under the laws of the humans as inscribed in the tomes of Plum Grove, the maximum punishment that I may impose is death by hanging."

Willis stared back at him, unblinking and defiant.

"You have taken the life of a fellow creature. You have used her and exploited her in all the ways that your kind will allow. You have worked her until she could work no longer, and when she was no longer of value to you, you alone passed judgment upon her and laid the flat steel of an axe against her skull."

The courtroom sat in hushed silence.

Judge Fogel continued, his voice crisp and forceful. "The crime of which you have been convicted is most worthy of the gallows."

At the defense table, Cyrus bowed his head. Beside him, Willis remained stone-faced.

Judge Fogel paused for a moment before the final condemnation. Then, his eyes seemed to grow soft and benevolent.

"Samuel Willis, the Animals have never sought vengeance. We have never sought your blood upon our hooves or your flesh upon our claws. For as long as we have walked this world together, we have asked only for the freedom to live beyond your chains and pens. Though you may decry us as lowly beasts, we harbor not the malice that stirs within you. Indeed, it is your heart alone that harbors such darkness to inspire the grim deeds this Court heard today. For this reason, the Court does not seek vengeance against you for the murder of Miss Ofelia or for the sins of the old ways."

At the words, the humans turned and looked

at each other, slack-jawed and perplexed. Across the aisle and in the jury box, the animals sat silently, placid and at peace. At the defense table, Willis' brow furrowed, and his face looked muddled.

Judge Fogel continued, his eyes never leaving the old man. "Samuel Willis, until the sun sets for eternity and the stars no longer rise above the town of Plum Grove, you shall never again return to your farm. The land belongs to you no more. Forevermore, the land belongs to the animals once enslaved there. This Court banishes you from the farm forever. In your stead, the animals shall live in peace. This is the sentence of the Court."

Willis sat dumbfounded and meek at the defense table, his eyes cast downward to the wooden floor. Beside him, Cyrus appeared equally startled. At the prosecution table, Tibbitts rested comfortably, only the faintest hint of satisfaction apparent beyond his otherwise stoic demeanor.

Judge Fogel banged his hoof on the bench three times. "This Court is dismissed."

Slowly and incredulously, the humans stood in their seats, quiet and subdued. Willis looked quizzically at Cyrus, who only nodded toward the double doors. The old man rose hesitantly and ambled toward the aisle, his legs wobbling beneath him as the humans watched in silence.

THE ANIMALS v. SAMUEL WILLIS

As Willis shuffled past the wooden benches, the animals stared straight ahead, their eyes averted and their gazes solemn. Cyrus followed quickly behind him.

When he reached the rear of the courtroom, he paused for a moment. To his right, Horace rested wearily against the wall. The little field mouse sat chittering atop the old donkey's head, towering above the chastened man who could do little more than bow his head and push through the double doors to the new world that lay beyond.

Thank you

Thank you for taking the time to read this book. If you found this reading worthwhile, please consider leaving a review wherever you purchased the book. More reviews will help more readers find and appreciate this story.

If you would like to explore my other books and receive a free short story based on the events of Chasing the Blue Sky, please visit :
www.lomackpublishing.com

Thank you again for giving your valuable time to read this book. I hope you found the time well-spent.

Will Lowrey

ABOUT THE AUTHOR

Will Lowrey is an attorney and animal rights advocate from Richmond, Virginia. He holds a Juris Doctor from Vermont Law School and a Bachelor of Science from Virginia Commonwealth University. For close to two decades, both before and after law school, Will has been actively involved in animal causes. His experiences include deployments to assist animals in disasters, the closure of roadside zoos, caring for animals from dog and cock fighting cases, community outreach for low income pet owners in areas ranging from urban neighborhoods to Native American reservations, animal rights protests, animal sheltering, public records campaigns against large institutions conducting animal research, and countless other adventures.

In 2018, Will founded Lomack Publishing (named after his first two rescued pit bulls) to promote the rights, interests, and dignity of animals through self-published literature. Will is the author of the novels *Chasing the Blue Sky* and *Where the Irises Bloom* along with several other animal-themed works. In addition, Will's legal article, *We the Pit*

Bull: The Fate of Pit Bulls Under the United States Constitution, is published in the Lewis and Clark Animal Law Review Journal, Volume 24, Issue 2.

While most of Will's writing focuses on animal causes, he has dabbled in other areas, writing *Simple Strategies for the Bar Exam*, a guide for law students and attorneys taking the bar exam, as well as *The Tenebrous Mind,* a collection of short horror stories.

Will enjoys hearing from readers. If you'd like to contact him, please visit:

www.lomackpublishing.com